the stories, like the characters, together despite their differences. And in all of the stories we also see the hint of 'Possibilities': the imagination which might just, now and then, take flight and escape expectations. *Now Batting for Boston* is a collection of stories that is, at heart, about the power of storytelling as a vehicle for hope and transformation."

Kathryn Conrad
Author of *Locked in the Family Cell:*
Gender, Sexuality, and Political
Agency in Irish National Discourse

Now Batting for Boston
More Stories by J. G. Hayes

HARRINGTON PARK PRESS
Southern Tier Editions
Gay Men's Fiction
Jay Quinn, Executive Editor

Elf Child by David M. Pierce

Huddle by Dan Boyle

The Man Pilot by James W. Ridout IV

Shadows of the Night: Queer Tales of the Uncanny and Unusual edited by Greg Herren

Van Allen's Ecstasy by Jim Tushinski

Beyond the Wind by Rob N. Hood

The Handsomest Man in the World by David Leddick

The Song of a Manchild by Durrell Owens

The Ice Sculptures: A Novel of Hollywood by Michael D. Craig

Between the Palms: A Collection of Gay Travel Erotica edited by Michael T. Luongo

Aura by Gary Glickman

Love Under Foot: An Erotic Celebration of Feet edited by Greg Wharton and M. Christian

The Tenth Man by E. William Podojil

Upon a Midnight Clear: Queer Christmas Tales edited by Greg Herren

Dryland's End by Felice Picano

Whose Eye Is on Which Sparrow? by Robert Taylor

Deep Water: A Sailor's Passage by E. M. Kahn

The Boys in the Brownstone by Kevin Scott

The Best of Both Worlds: Bisexual Erotica edited by Sage Vivant and M. Christian

Some Dance to Remember: A Memoir-Novel of San Francisco, 1970-1982 by Jack Fritscher

Confessions of a Male Nurse by Richard S. Ferri

The Millionaire of Love by David Leddick

Transgender Erotica: Trans Figures edited by M. Christian

Skip Macalester by J. E. Robinson

Chemistry by Lewis DeSimone

Friends, Lovers, and Roses by Vernon Clay

Beyond Machu by William Maltese

Virginia Bedfellows by Gavin Morris

Now Batting for Boston: More Stories by J. G. Hayes by J. G. Hayes

Now Batting for Boston
More Stories by J. G. Hayes

J. G. Hayes

Southern Tier Editions™
Harrington Park Press®
An Imprint of The Haworth Press, Inc.
New York • London • Oxford

For more information on this book or to order, visit
http://www.haworthpress.com/store/product.asp?sku=5174

or call 1-800-HAWORTH (800-429-6784) in the United States and Canada
or (607) 722-5857 outside the United States and Canada

or contact orders@HaworthPress.com

Published by

Southern Tier Editions™, Harrington Park Press®, an imprint of The Haworth Press, Inc.,
10 Alice Street, Binghamton, NY 13904-1580.

PUBLISHER'S NOTE
This is a work of fiction. Names, characters, places, and incidents either are the products of the author's imagination or are used fictitiously, and any resemblance to actual persons, living or dead, business establishments, events, or locales is entirely coincidental.

Cover photos of the late Franky Hayes and his son, author J. G. Hayes, both at the age of eighteen.

Cover design by Lora Wiggins.

Library of Congress Cataloging-in-Publication Data

Hayes, J. G. (Joseph George), 1965-
    Now batting for Boston : more stories by J.G. Hayes / J.G. Hayes.
        p. ; cm.
    ISBN-13: 978-1-56023-522-4
    ISBN-10: 1-56023-522-5 (pbk. : alk. paper)
    1. South Boston (Boston, Mass.)—Fiction. 2. Irish American families—Fiction. 3. Working class families—Fiction. 4. Catholics—Fiction. 5. Gay youth—Fiction. I. Title.

PS3608.A93N69 2005
813'.6—dc22
                                                                                    2005001147

To Vonn, and Davey, and my mother

CONTENTS

Preface

One reviewer of my book *This Thing Called Courage: South Boston Stories* (2002) called the collection "often bleak but always moving." That "B" word gave me pause, for ostensibly if there were one thing I should like to impart to readers, it is hope. Going through the stories after that assessment, I did find that many of the characters suffered untimely demises, and I wondered if I had unintentionally added to the still prevalent bromide, *if they're gay they have to die.* My conclusion is that this was coincidental: In a five-year period, over 350 young men had died in South Boston due to a variety of causes—alcohol and drug overdose, violence, and suicide. To have portrayed otherwise in my stories would have been a disservice to the reality of an often bleak situation. Above and beyond telling stories that I felt needed to be told, my intention, if I am pressed to confess to one, would have been to highlight the ill effects of the violence caused by homophobia, whether it comes from family, peers, church, school, media, advertising, or consumerist/corporate culture. Although these new stories were written at the same time as the tales in the previous collection, some, hopefully, are less bleak. In many ways, we author our own futures, regardless of whether we know it; if we have learned one thing, it is how to survive. Perhaps now it's time to live. Here's to getting the guy in the end, especially if we find the one we have been searching for all along is a recovered, empowered self.

Acknowledgments

The author would like to express his appreciation to all who made this second collection of short stories possible. So many people are involved in this process that some are inevitably unmentioned; I would like to acknowledge these people first. Numerous people, from Wales to New South Wales, from South Africa to South Boston, wrote to me following the publication of *This Thing Called Courage: South Boston Stories,* and their words of encouragement will never be forgotten. Among this group I would like to acknowledge Bron Bateman, Tom O'Leary, Grady Harp, Jim Cooper, Jonathan Cassie, Jamie O'Neill (of brilliant *At Swim Two Boys* fame), and especially W. Perry Barton, whose initial contact has led to a deep and abiding friendship and a source of continual support. Paul and Warren of We Think the World of You bookstore, and John Mitzel of Calamus Books have been unflagging supporters of my work, as have been Jay Quinn, Bill Palmer, and Bill Cohen; my appreciation cannot be adequately expressed in words. The Honorable Dermot Meagher has been a one-man publicity department, as well as a source of encouragement, love, and friendship. Tom Lee, Vonn Moore, and Dave Sullivan contributed in ways too numerous to mention, but suffice it to say that on many occasions the writing process would have slid to a halt were it not for them. That goes as well for my family, and also, especially, to Davey in Ann Arbor. I am in the unfamiliar position of being rendered wordless at how much your support and love have meant to me. Ditto for the Great Creator, the source of all big C and little c creation.

Now Batting for Boston . . .

When what was left of my father slid back from World War II, his mangled body and frazzled mind lay wrapped in gauze below decks on a vast Navy hospital ship. The USS *Salem* steamed ponderously from New Guinea to San Francisco Bay, protected by a veritable barnyard of watchful mother hens with attitude: destroyers, battleships, antiaircraft cruisers, and PT boats. The voyage took forty-two queasy days. My father was labeled 100 percent disabled because of what had happened to him.

Dad, what happened to you? What happened to you over there in the war?

On the trip home, Dad said later, so many men on his ship ended their physical suffering, or forestalled post-traumatic stress syndrome, by jumping to their screaming deaths into the Pacific, that all still-living patients were shot up with morphine so they'd sleep until they reached America. Presumably, everything would be okay once they reached home.

I got hurt.

When he reached California, my father had two years in a VA hospital bed to contemplate what he would do with his life, now that his life as he had known it seemed over.

He was twenty years old.

He went over the options in his head:

He could spend the rest of his life in VA hospitals (this was the course his doctors recommended); or he could return to civilian life, living on the small but lifelong pension 100 percent disabled veterans were entitled to; but what then? The Depression had hit when he was in the sixth grade, and his spouseless mother had yanked him out of school, he being the oldest, to support the rest of the family by mop-ping floors nights at the Waldorf Diner. He had no education, no skills. The GI Bill provided education for returning vets, but his lingering malaria and dengue fever gave him all the physical symptoms of Tourette's syndrome, making daily interactions difficult.

He was not encouraged to further his education. Those were not times when those perceived to be other-abled were welcomed—or in most cases even allowed—to dip into the largesse of post–World War II American society and its institutions.

But how, Dad? How? Do you got any medals? Were you a hero? Did you shoot anybody?

Baseball was no longer an option for my father. Until the war, it had been the only one. In fact, Dad had been signed to a minor league contract by the Boston Braves, which seemed at the time not only the culmination of a lifelong dream, but a ticket to Life itself, in all its shining promise. But two months after being signed he was drafted into the Army, and fourteen months after that he—or more accurately someone who had once been him—was on his way home on a hospital ship, his body burned and filleted with knife wounds, his nervous system shredded by malaria, dengue fever, and trauma.

When he was able to sit up in a wheelchair, my father would ask the pretty nurse to push him to the fourth-floor window of the VA hospital in San Francisco. There he would sit for hours and gaze at Life beyond the hospital grounds. Life with all its postwar rush, its hope of forgetfulness and reward, its promise of prosperity. Life seemed a river that did not stop at that particular VA hospital. And my father would sit there and gaze at it rushing by.

A hero? Naw, I wasn't no hero. How did I get hurt? Well . . . maybe when you kids are older—

It was the lights that finally got to him, he would tell us later. The lights of San Francisco at night. They reminded him of the Christmases he'd never known as a child, but had always dreamed of. Somewhere out there amid all that light, he thought, there was Something for him. Someone, maybe. So he abandoned the life of the hospital pensioner, although most said he shouldn't. In fact he was discharged *AMA,* Against Medical Advice. He left on Christmas Eve, when the city of San Francisco seemed ablaze with light.

And so my father returned at last to South Boston, with its odd gravitational pull, which, if it doesn't get the body, always seems to get the mind. He found pity there in his hometown, and sympathy, and free drinks at the Disabled American Veterans post, but little else. The baseball fields of his youth seemed like graveyards now, overflowing with all his rotting dreams, and these fields he'd avoid if he could, or hobble by quickly with his head down if he couldn't. His life felt empty. Something (possibly all things) was missing. And so he found himself one night at the Shrine to Saint Anthony, behind the gothic neighborhood church that once had been his own.

Dad, c'mon. We're older now. You can tell us. What happened to you?

There were two things they'd said about Franky Hayes in his prewar youth: that he was one of the nicest-looking guys in Southie, and that he was its greatest ballplayer. Scarred, limping, spastic and shattered, he would not parade these two ghosts in front of his old twelve o'clock-Mass congregation. There were already enough un-seen spirits—the hundreds who wouldn't be coming home. But just outside this church, to the rear, tucked in a half-forgotten, tree-shrouded corner, was a shrine to Saint Anthony. A six-foot marble statue of the saint, holding the infant Jesus, sat in the midst of roses and lilies lovingly tended twice weekly by rosary-garbling ancient women. You could almost shovel the anguish there, Dad said; the air was that thick with it, the hope, the faith, the joy of a prayer an-swered, the grief of WE-REGRET-TO-INFORM-YOU telegrams carefully peeled open with callused hands and dirty fingernails under the sym-pathetic scent of lilies and roses. And there, one desperate midnight, my father presented his petition to the patron saint of lost things.

We were the first battalion on New Guinea. The machine-gun nests were killing us; we were dropping like flies. Jimmy Kiley was right next to me when . . . never mind. It was our job to find out the location of those nests, and radio them back to the battleships.

My father, other-abled and shattered as he was, dared to pray for a helper that night at the shrine—a mate, someone he could share his life with. He vowed that should his prayer be answered, this woman would not be old before her time. She would be his queen, and, disabled as he was, he would treat her with all the love, help, and devotion he could.

Within a month my father met my mother, on a blind date that both of them tried to wrangle out of at the last minute. They eloped within two months, my suburban mother guessing, rightly, that this still handsome but uneducated, unskilled fast-talker would never be good enough for her upward-bound middle-class family. Within a year she was back at her family's suburban domicile, under virtual house arrest, with a golden-haired, brown-eyed daughter. Her parents tried to get the marriage annulled. Somehow my father got hold of a priest's cassock and collar. He dressed his best friend Pinky McGill in them, then sent him to my mother's people's God-fearing house, where the most casual utterance of any priest was thought to have fallen from the lips of The Almighty Himself.

"For shame at trying to break up God's Holy Union!" the faux priest finger-pointed at my quaking grandparents, as he hustled my mother and oldest sister out the door and back to my father, who was waiting in the car down the street, laughing and smoking a Chesterfield cigarette, his feet up on the dashboard.

We fanned out through the jungle, wrapped in camouflage. Somehow I got separated from the others. I fell into this pit, about twelve feet deep—I guess it was kind of a booby trap. I broke my leg when I landed. I couldn't get out. By day we owned the jungle, with support from the artillery. But at night it was a different story. That night the enemy came, checking on their traps. And so they found me.

My father kept his vow. He put his children to bed each night, mesmerizing us with his impromptu stories that kicked down the borders of our imaginations. He washed the dishes after every meal, and cooked when my mother was too tired. And while other women in our neighborhood grew wrinkled and bitter with endless children and chores, our mother stayed young and smiling, warmed by the notes Dad would leave for her on the kitchen table each morning, notes that always began, "To My Beautiful Queen, Heaven-sent from above, the answer to My Prayer . . ."

They had nothing in common. In forty-nine years of marriage, it was never established who ruled the roost—not for a lack of trying.

They fought over money and my father's monthly drinking binges or his refusal to ever wear a necktie, my mother's exorbitant phone bills, the in-laws that Dad called insufferable snobs, and Mom deemed Wild Irish Rebels.

But their love for each other—instant, inexplicable, wild—never waned. And even in the midst of a fight, they couldn't pass each other without stopping, snarling, and then a look, a linger, and soon they would retreat to the bedroom.

I think there was only one of them who came that first night. There was a shadow above me at the roof of the pit, and then there was a noise, and another shadow passed over the first one, darker. I was waiting for him, but still he surprised me, getting me with his knife. No one'd dare use a gun; both sides were too close. Jungle fighting's always done with a knife.

He'd look at his hands, the deft fingers, maybe wondering how these instruments that had been finely tuned to excel at a pastime had been transformed into instruments of killing. He'd shove them behind his back, always, and look at us with eyes that made us wish we never asked. Then he'd always have to touch us, rumpling our hair, pulling us into the hushed stadium of his arms, as if renewing some pledge that his hands would kill no more, but only soothe from now on, only play.

He'd gather us up summer nights and Sundays and we'd half-walk/half-run the several blocks to the park, the August ground so dusty clouds of powder would sift up when we ran across the infield, filling our hand-me-down sneakers as if we were trudging along the ocean floor down at City Point Beach. Dad couldn't do much more than pitch, and as we got older we took even that chore away from him. Then he'd stand on the sidelines orchestrating scenarios *(man on second nobody out bottom of the sixth, bases loaded last of the ninth),* pulling from his back pocket the wire kitchen strainer he'd pilfered from Mom against her wishes. He'd hold it up to his mouth as if it was a microphone, then introduce each one of us as we stepped up to the plate to an imagined throng filling the moth-skimmed summer air.

"Now batting for Boston," he'd intone in an affected voice booming with urgency, "now batting for Boston, the center fielder, Hayes . . ."

Some days I'd be good. Some days I'd be unstoppable, flowing like electricity, vaulted up into a high blue place where fantasy and reality blended, then exploded, and there was nothing I couldn't do. But other days there would be purple clover growing between my tattered sneakers, and I'd have to pick a bunch for Mom; or maybe I'd see a cloud in the sky that needed only a turret here and a drawbridge there to turn it back into a castle; or sometimes there'd be a butterfly between first and second, sipping nectar with an exquisite salmon tongue the size of a pinhead, its body pulsing in delight, and a ball would scoot between my surprised scraped legs, or jiggle just beyond my desperate reach. And I'd look up at Dad, half in defiance, half in shame. And as my brothers and I grew stronger, taller, leaner, and the sweat of our bodies took on a surprising, goaty tang, baseball became more than a game, and the prize nothing less than my Dad's affection and interest.

Compared to my older brothers, I was good, but not the best. And with the prize being my father's love, there was no room, in my mind anyway, for anything less.

You're the best hitter in the bunch, Joey, when you concentrate. Why won't you concentrate?

I don't want to, I'd say, kicking up the dust with a sneaker. *How the fuck do I know?* I wanted to say, *it's your gene pool.* I wasn't like the others. There were whole weeks when I was Normal, then something would click and I'd be off painting whole walls with murals, filling frenzied notebooks with my stories, wandering the abandoned railroad tracks, or climbing the piles of rubbish down at the junkyard, in search of something I couldn't name.

The summer between my thirteenth and fourteenth years, I grew to my adult height in two explosive months, and the following school year I began pitching. In two years I never lost a game, and scouts began to come to watch not only me but one of my older brothers as well. But still the wildness within me grew along with my body—the belief, the hope, that there was an entire other world beyond the confines of baseball, beyond the borders of South Boston.

I quit baseball in the middle of a game at sixteen, in a bat-throwing, explosive rage that shocked everyone there—myself and my father included. We walked home along the buckling sidewalks in silence, my father grim-eyed and sorrowful, reliving his own sorry separation from baseball; and me, two steps behind him, defiantly popping the buttons from my dirty uniform. I had a passion for baseball my siblings, adept as they were, did not possess. But I was declaring my independence from a world in which a father's affection was doled out in proportion to a son's ability to play ball. It wasn't right, and like so many others before me, I sank my own ship, colors waving high. Our walk home was a funeral march, and we both knew it.

We couldn't help who we were, and what had happened to us.

AS A YOUNG MAN, I would go up to the roof of the housing project we lived in, and stare out at the lights of the nearby city. Life was out there, something separate and Other from what I was living then. Like my father before me, I dreamed of the life I might find in those lights. I would recall my father's mother's words, that I was the only one among his children that resembled him in his youth. And also like my father, I had a love for the game of baseball that was more than idle pleasure: it was poetry, beauty, symmetry, a swirl of green and white and youth and summer forever frozen into a transcending perfection . . .

But unlike my father, it wasn't only Life I hoped to jump into during my long light-gazing vigils on the roof. In particular it was a particular bar in a particular part of town, a bar whose blacked-out front windows were lit up like Christmas every day of the year. It was a bar for people like me. For although I may have looked like my father, and loved baseball like my father, I was not heterosexual like my father. And all the prayers to Saint Anthony in the world hadn't changed that.

I GOT THE BAR'S ADDRESS from a newspaper clipping, torn and yellowed after being under my mattress for three years. Each Christmas Eve I would try to go, but always chicken out at the last minute, sometimes vomiting from nervousness as I watched outside from my pickup truck, engine running.

I'd explode at my friends at the cavalier way they'd take their girlfriends or young wives for granted—lying, cheating, sometimes slapping. They didn't know how lucky they were, how privileged, to not only walk down the street holding someone's hand, take someone out on a date, and enjoy what would follow after, but to have someone, to look into someone's eyes without faking or hiding their true feelings. For I, too, like my father before me, had taken a vow, that if I was sent someone, I would never forget the gift I'd been given. And at eighteen I *knew* that if I ever got the courage to go into that bar, that bar for people like me, I would quickly find the one I'd been waiting for all my life, someone with whom I could share my life. Maybe on the first night, perhaps the second, but certainly by the third or fourth visit at the latest.

I really believed that.

I had to. There was nothing else to hold on to during those years.

IT WAS A CHRISTMAS EVE two years later when I found him. The place wasn't crowded, which is why I had the nerve to stay there once I got inside. Like me, he had marooned himself into a shadowed corner. He looked scared, unsure, gazing down at his large work boots. We quick-stared at each other through three label-peeled beers until we finally got the nerve to edge closer to each other; closer; closer still. When we finally began to talk, I became lost in the light of his eyes, and for once didn't have to worry about what my own eyes might be saying.

WHEN THEY FOUND my father at the bottom of the jungle pit five days after he'd fallen into it, his body was riddled with knife wounds. Five dead Japanese soldiers were lying with him, like silent attendants. Second-degree burns covered 80 percent of Dad's body. He told us he kept himself sane and alive by replaying in his head favorite ball games from his youth, play by play, batter by batter, crowd-roar by crowd-roar.

But what happened, Dad? What happened? How'd them Japs get there? Did you kill them all? How did you get burned?

He'd never give us any details. The glib facade would fade for a moment, the hazel eyes shuttering open for once. *They hurt me,* he'd say. Nothing more.

They hurt me.

I BROUGHT THE YOUNG MAN home to my apartment that first night because I knew he was the one, the one I'd been dreaming about all my life. Sometimes you just know. Two years older than I, he was a football coach for a suburban high school south of Boston, and the loneliness and hope that I thought I saw in his river-blue eyes were an invitation to try to heal his wounds, and my own at the same time. Sister Louisa in third grade had told us "You get into heaven two at a time; you've got to take someone with you." I thought I finally understood what she meant.

I found Life in the bed that night, Life in all its glory and madness, in tangled passion I never knew I could feel. And when the morning light found him sleeping in my arms, I had to go downstairs to the kitchen so he wouldn't see me crying.

I decided I'd make us Christmas breakfast. The kitchen clock was the same; the wallpaper too. But everything was entirely different, for upstairs in my bed, waiting for me with sleeping intention, was someone of my own, someone I could share my life with, someone I'd grow with. And we'd both be better for it, learning as much about ourselves as we'd learn about each other.

I practiced the words I would say to him as I ascended the stairs, how I would let him know I'd been waiting all my life for this. Tricky but truthful words that would indicate, but not scare off. We are never content with just the experiences of our lives; we must talk about them too.

When I pushed open the bedroom door with a bare foot, the breakfast tray in my hands, he was pulling on his rumpled clothes. He avoided my eyes as he dressed, a modest stranger in a locker room.

"I ahh . . . made us some breakfast."

"Oh . . . thanks, but I gotta go." His sweater covered up the smooth mounds of his shoulders.

"Oh. Ahh . . . where?"

"Christmas dinner. I gotta be somewhere by noontime." He made eye contact at last, smiled weakly, then began extracting his socks and shoes, mixed up with mine, from the foot of the bed.

"What . . . what time will you be back?" I asked. People didn't do what we had done the night before without some tacit understanding that they were now a couple, did they?

"Back?" he asked, his voice sincere with curiosity.

Something cold began squirting inside my stomach.

"Back . . . here," I said.

He cocked his head to the side, the way a dog will when you say an unfamiliar word to it.

"Ahh, look . . . John, I—"

"It's Joe."

"Oh—sorry, Joe. Look, I gotta get back home. My lover'll be back from his parents soon and I need to be home before he is."

"Your . . . lover?"

"Yeah," he answered, beads of annoyance strung along the thread of his voice.

"Well, I. . . . I mean, if you have a lover, how come we. . . . I mean, why did you—"

"You were just too good to resist, hot stuff," he said, smiling tightly, like this was a line he'd grown tired of repeating. He put one foot, then the other, up on the rumpled sheets to tie his boots.

"Thanks for everything," he said, grabbing his coat. "See you out and about, probably." He snatched a piece of toast from the tray I still held as he left the bedroom. A minute later, still holding the tray, I heard his car start up and rumble out of the driveway.

WHEN MY FATHER DIED some years later, I was at the gym. I inexplicably stopped in the middle of my workout, didn't even change, and drove directly to my parents' house. I passed through their kitchen, my breeze fluttering a morning note on the table from Dad to Mom which began, "To my honey . . ." I climbed the stairs to my father's bedroom with a baby-grand lump of dread upon my back. He had been in good health, but somehow I knew. I think he must have called me to his house that day.

I knocked on the closed bedroom door. I knew I'd get no answer, and I didn't. I opened the door. He was half-in and half-out of his bed. *Dad? Dad?* It looked like he had tried to get out of the bed, then fallen back. *Dad?* I walked over to him, reached out a shaking hand. I touched him. He was dead. *Dad! Dad! Oh, God—Dad!*

IT'S NOT CHRISTMAS MORNING but it's close enough. I awake to find a younger man sleeping next to me in my bed. I think hard, trying to dredge up his name from the landfill of last night. At length I do. But what of that? What it's really time for now is a glass of water, a pause, a pondering of that elusive truth that still lies elsewhere, beyond this rumpled bed. I do this so seldom—and now I remember why.

Suddenly, elbow propped, he's staring at me in rapt appraisal something else I vaguely remember (or disremember, as they say down South) in his oddly familiar eyes.

"Good morning," he coos sleepily. Ever alert for such trivialities (my Early Warning Defense System, as it were), I notice his breath smells swampy, and he's got a tiny blackhead in his right ear. "The first of many, I hope," he continues, coming in too close. Something in his tone sets me on edge. *You don't even know me,* I think. *Or maybe you know me too well.* I look at my watch.

"Well, I gotta get going," I lie.

His face blurs into another mood, a portrait someone's thrown water on.

"Oh. Where . . . wha—"

"I've got a lot of stuff to do today," I explain. I jump out of bed and pull on a pair of plaid boxers that I paid eighteen dollars for, just for occasions like this.

"Oh."

I say nothing. I'm waiting for the other shoe to drop.

"Do you. . . . Maybe we can get together someti—"

"Look, Ken," I say. "We had a great night. Really, it was . . . great. But I'm not really . . . I'm not really looking to get involved right now. With . . . anyone. I got a lot going on in my life right now."

"It's Kent," he mumbles.

I WATCH HIM from my bedroom window exactly three minutes later. He brushes the snow off his blue, generic car in red-handed, gloveless chops. Then he hops in, starts it up, and pulls away.

"Welcome to the big leagues, kid," I mutter, pulling down my shade.

LATER IN THE DAY I visit Dad's grave. We have these little talks, you see: I can tell him everything, now that he's gone. I tell him what a shitty year the Red Sox had, again, but how brilliantly they broke our hearts *this* time. We engage in small talk for a bit. Then he looks right through me.

"Another one-nighter last night, huh Joe?" he asks. "*Quo vadis,* kiddo? Where's all this getting you?"

I fidget, make a face, fold my arms across my chest.

"You writing a book?" I ask.

He doesn't laugh.

"Still the wise guy, huh Joe?"

"I learned from the master," I reply. Silence.

"Well? Tell me," he says. "I'm still your father, even if I am dead."

"So what if I did?" I finally blurt. "It's a free country."

"I always hated it when you'd say that as a kid."

"Well, it's true, Dad."

"Maybe," he says. "But there's no such thing as a free lunch."

There's a long pause. The wind curls around the cement-colored branches of the bare trees, making an empty sound. Dad looks right through me again, seeing my insides, which feel vacant except for the residue of something long broken, like solidified egg yolk, yellowed and dried now—sterile, useless, but clinging still.

What happened to you, Joe? he asks. *The boy who was gonna be president? The one who dreamed of just one person in his life, forever? My boy. My son. What happened to you?*

I sigh. A long one.

You wouldn't understand, Dad.

Of course I would. C'mon, tell me, Joe. What happened to you?

I close my eyes, stare him in the face. I lie down on his grave, stretch my arms out.

They hurt me, Dad, I whisper, the snow cold against my mouth.

They hurt me.

Once on Christmas Eve

Christmas Eve, and five of us were in a bar—separately. Christmas can unify, they say, but not on this night, not for us anyway. We must have been the equal and opposite effect for all the red-and-white happiness that glittered elsewhere, beyond these walls.

There was the bartender, watching the blare of a basketball game on the television perched at the bar's end. There was an overweight businessman three stools down from me, whose angle of slumping declination decreased with each drink. On the last stool sat a senior citizen, that most forlorn of gay-bar denizens, sitting in shadow. Everything he owned seemed to have withered, except his eyes—these still burned with something. They had caught mine in the mirror once and that had been enough. Dust and ashes, ashes and dust . . . I had seen my future. Provided I survived the plague, of course.

Provided I survived this night.

The mid-thirtiesish guy (my own age), was four stools down on my other side. I had felt the bitterness of the evening falling from the folds of his tweed overcoat when he entered some twenty minutes earlier. He was still wrapped loosely in the coat, and upon his lap sat a large box done up in red and gold Christmas foil, with a now-crushed green bow on top. Like the rest of us, he was keeping his eyes frozen forward.

Dizzy strings of red bulbs crisscrossed the smoky ceiling. Multicolored lights chased each other around the edges of the bar's plate-glass mirror. Holiday music set to a frenzied disco beat thumped across the empty dance floor behind us, mourning those who weren't here, mocking those who were. As the songs, and their lyrics, played on, my reaction went from amused irony to an almost sweating desperation.

The businessman shook to life to order another drink. The bartender grudgingly obliged. I got the feeling *he* had somewhere else to go this evening, unlike, apparently, the rest of us. I turned my eyes downward in the face of his scorn, but I raised my finger nonetheless for another shot of oblivion. And yet I never could quite get there.

Maybe the holidays' nastiest trick is its command to recall, to relive, to remember. With alcohol greasing the skids, my mind slid back thirty years, stopping at a long-ago Christmas the way a jukebox set at random yanks out a selection totally unexpected, but all too familiar. For quickly I was five again, and stepping out our old back door into a world made dazzling and supreme by a foot of snow the night before. It was Christmas Day in my reverie, and neither impassable roads nor a passel of young children would stop my parents from bundling us all up to go out to Aunt Anne's in the country. Suddenly they were all with me, spilling out the door. I could hear their voices—Mom's clear laugh, Dad still young and handsome, and alive, picking out targets for brother Bob to hit with snowballs, the girls gushing over the clothes and dolls they'd just received, and me, the youngest at the time, shocked into muteness by the triple sublimity of it all: a snowstorm, Christmas Day, and an upcoming ride on the numinous subway all on the same day. Everything was a kaleidoscope of delight that grew as the day unfurled like a flower, from the new snow-white coats of the too-tall pines, to the racehorse game my mother magically produced from her bag once we were tucked into our rumbling subway seats.

And then Aunt Anne's, a gaggle of relations hugging me, wizened old relatives to mesmerize me with their tales, strange new cousins to play with, the smell of forty different delights melding into one in Aunt Anne's kitchen: slow-basted turkey, gingerbread, orange peel upon the fire, bubbling cinnamon cider that coated the windows as its fragrance filled the house. And Aunt Anne's secret stairway that led up to the attic, where still-wrapped presents for her favorite nephews and nieces lay before our rapacious eyes like just-discovered continents, limitless in their potential. And then from downstairs somewhere came the holy sound of Singing, Singing, the sound of singing and I felt there was singing throughout the universe . . .

BACK AT THE BAR now.

My eyes refocus and I see the young man in the overcoat, his handsome profile reflected in the mirror, staring down at nothing. His gaily wrapped package by this time has fallen on the floor, and I get the feeling it's doomed to stay there, treasure at the bottom of a frozen sea. And he's crying. Softly, almost silently, yet somehow this sound rises above the dueling cacophony of the television and the music. And it seems no one else can hear this.

But say what you will about the holidays, they do give us license, if we will but take it; the excuse to do, if not great things, then good things. So because it was Christmas Eve and I could get away with it, I abandoned my barstool and approached the crying young man.

I sat down on the squishy stool next to his.

We stared forward at our own solemn reflections. He kept up his quiet crying, but—Christmas miracle—we reached for each other, and our hands met and clasped halfway along the immeasurable distance between us.

Silently we sat, hand in hand, staring straight ahead, the din of the disco and the drone of the television falling hard all around us, holding back the horror of this night. And still he cried.

At last he turned to me. I turned to him. We stared at each other for a moment. Then he smiled and reached down to the ground to retrieve his package. He handed it to me.

"Merry Christmas," he said.

There Is a Balm in Gilead

The person who did the cleaning every Wednesday afternoon had just finished, but you checked the rooms anyway—all of them. Nine of them, if you counted the small study on the second floor, and you always did. A lot of rooms for the Back Bay. You put your glasses on to make sure everything was in order, that everything was spotless. You consulted the antique marble clock on the living room mantel. It said you still had forty-five minutes before he came, but with all you had to do you thought rushing at the last minute would prove catastrophic.

You hadn't seen him in eight years.

You decided on the upstairs bathroom for your shower. That was the master bedroom's shower, closer to the dressing room. It was nearly as large as the flat you had grown up in; you measured it your second day here three years ago. It was done in large slate-blue tiles and golden walls with an orange wash stippled over them—somehow it reminded you of an Enya album cover every time you were in there. You stripped in the dressing room, threw your dirty clothes onto the closet floor.

There were many soap and shampoo and conditioner choices in the built-in shower caddy beside you, but you made your selections instantly, decisively, without any of your usual hesitations. The lavender-musk body wash; the chamomile shampoo; the evening primrose finishing conditioner.

You got half-hard while you showered. You tried to assign this to the primitive herbal smells, the slippery feel of the gel as you washed, and not the fact that you would see him in less than an hour. As you washed your chest, a memory bashed you: One night in the D Street bedroom, the moon full or close enough, he had risen from the bed, opened the blinds and windows, had come naked back to you. *I want moon air in here,* he told you. *I want to see you washed in moon air.* You wondered, why this one, why this particular memory as opposed to ten thousand others. Maybe because it had been one of the only times he had been poetic, had given vent to the poetry that you always knew sang within him.

You gritted your teeth, closed your eyes, pressed your hands against the shower wall. To hold back the memories, to push them back. You were careful to spray the sudsy residue off the gleaming stone-tile walls when you finished.

What lay before you this evening could never be construed as anything other than work—difficult, soul-wrenching—but still you luxuriated in the feel of the Egyptian cotton towel, half the size of a bedspread. When you finished drying you stood naked before the full-length teak-framed mirror at the bathroom's other end, just beyond the marble Jacuzzi tub. You examined your body minutely; you turned around, you walked away from the mirror with your head turned over your shoulder. You flexed, your face serious. You saw that you still had it; thirty-eight but you still had it. The hair as red as ever, the skin as taut and smooth. Tauter now with a bit more muscle, if anything, you told yourself. You still had it. Amazing after all the things your body had been through, you thought. You thanked God for your body, for the miracle it was, the miracle of life. But you thanked him more for your sobriety.

You put on the Armani suit. You worried this might be too much—but it would impress him, and all week you had planned on wearing it, all week, ever since his phone call. You stuck with the Armani but you didn't wear the tie.

You dressed left; it showed through the suit. Not to the point of being featured but just enough for him to notice—of course he would notice. But what of that? The shoes pinched a little, but that was nothing. Three-hundred dollar shoes, but they pinched a little.

You checked all the rooms again. You left all the windows open halfway, exactly. You always did when the weather allowed and you noticed how the June city twilight breeze puffed the velvet curtains in some of the rooms but not others. The rooms took on a diffused pink-and-orange glow. You hoped the long twilight, the sounds of the trees all whispering just outside, would last. You lit certain soft lamps in rooms on the first floor. The place had never looked better. You thought how the intangibles were cooperating with you tonight. That was good; you would need all the help you could get.

You prayed to your Higher Power. You weren't sure you were doing the right thing, but your higher aim was noble.

You got an ice bucket from under the kitchen sink. It wasn't dusty but you rinsed it anyway. You remembered a priest you had known when you were seventeen who had given you a silver ice bucket that year as a Christmas present. You thought at the time what an odd gift that was. You still thought that. You filled it halfway with ice from the automatic dispenser at the stainless-steel Sub-Zero refrigerator. You recalled how you'd stolen a look at your father's pay stub when you were seven; he had grossed that year several hundred dollars less than this refrigerator had cost two months ago.

You hurried out into the hall and left the ice bucket on the bottom step of the maroon-carpeted winding stairway. You bounded upstairs two at a time for the Listerine. You rinsed your mouth out. You had gotten a little sun that morning, just enough so that, in the mirror, you glowed. A very small drop of the mouthwash dribbled onto the Armani suit. You blotted it away with a wet tissue. It didn't stain. You went back downstairs.

You brought the ice bucket out into the parlor. It was a double parlor but you put the far light on, over the ferns at the bay window, to make the room look even larger. This is where it would happen, where you would confront the past, him. Heal the past, maybe, heal the both of you. It was two days before the solstice and the long summer twilight infused the room with a vermilion-tangerine light that came from nowhere, everywhere. The room looked plaintive, almost beseeching, in this light, and you wondered if you could take it. You placed the ice bucket onto the mahogany table, moored among the leather sofas. You put one can of diet cola and one imported beer into the ice bucket.

You looked at the clock at the same time the doorbell rang. Of course he was still punctual. Your heart leapt up; he had held empire over you for almost thirty years and your heart still leapt up. You made yourself sit still until you counted to thirty, and this reminded you of "this has been a test of the emergency broadcast system" announcements on the radio when you were both young, when you and he had held your breaths during the blare signal in case the Communists attacked with bombs.

You counted to thirty after you heard the buzzer, to set the tone. You would set the tone throughout the evening, and this was the necessary beginning. You couldn't appear anxious at all. You had come too far. You knew he wouldn't ring the buzzer again and he didn't, not when he had gotten a look at the imposing front of the brownstone. Wealth had always impressed him, intimidated him.

That was the problem.

You made yourself smile before you opened the door.

"Tim," you said, half dropping your eyelids. You congratulated yourself on this gesture. It was unplanned but perfect; he might have been the neighbor you saw twice a year and that was enough. You extended your hand and wondered how you didn't drop.

"Not *Timmy?*" he asked, and as usual his question caught you unawares, but you'd had years to practice hiding this. His eyes were still as blue as your dreams remembered, that recurring dream in which his eyes turned into waterfalls. There was still one way that his eyes looked and you wanted to hurt him for it, belittle him; a second later they were different, and you wanted to hold him forever. You examined these feelings and found they ran into each other, like a prism of color. One became the other and you couldn't say where, how.

"Tim, Timmy," you said. You shrugged. "You're still Timmy?" and you turned it around on him, you had hoped you would. "Ahh . . . come on in." His eyes took in the place at a glance and they swelled. They ran through the foyer into the continent of rooms beyond, then back to you. He smirked when he caught you watching him; you knew he hated thinking you had caught him being impressed. But who wouldn't be impressed? You almost laughed at the joy of seeing him, the absurdity of the role you had donned for this evening.

"Nice place," he said quietly as you led him into the parlor. You couldn't help smiling at the astonishment in his voice, the envy, but at the same time you begged saints that he wouldn't be poignant tonight. You thought silence and poignancy out of him would be the end of you.

When you got to the middle of the room where the sofas were, he was still looking around, almost slack-jawed. There was so much to take in, the baby grand in the next room, the antique silk-watered wallpaper, the hand-painted pilasters; but still his eyes kept smashing back to you and you thought of consumption, of something being consumed every time he looked at you. Still. You remembered yourself, broke into a smile.

"Jeez, you look *great*," you said, taking a seat opposite him. The two kid-leather sofas you were seated on were separated only by the mahogany table, inlaid with ivory, but neither of you were leaning forward yet. On the contrary, you were eyeing each other like opponents before a boxing match, you thought—ramrod straight and backs pressed against the leather. He was wearing black microfiber pants and a short-sleeved periwinkle shirt with the top two buttons undone, but undone in a subtle way. Only he could manage something that like. It was a brilliant color on him and the light in the room flew to it, but still his eyes mocked it. The shirt couldn't compete with his eyes; what shirt ever could? You could see the first tufts of his auburn chest hair, the chest hairs you had counted one night while he laid back and laughed at you. You had counted them from his collarbone all the way down to . . . to . . .

The hair of his head was still chestnut, and for a quick second a part of you wanted to haul him outside so you could see, again, what the sun did to his hair. You remembered how the sun on his hair had always arrested you, always crushed whatever else you had been thinking of. You looked at the hand-carved grandfather clock for reassurance and wondered whether you were more what you wanted to do, or more what you should do, and why these disparate parts of you were sometimes at each other's throats. But you looked again at his hair and saw silver strands on the side—only a few. You recalled how you had longed for this day, longed for the time when the aging process would wipe its loving hands across him and how this might show him that your love of him was pure, everlasting, and not dependent upon his looks alone. That was how much you had loved him, and you had longed for this day so you could show this to him, share this with him.

That was a long time ago.

You prayed he hadn't become Republican, hadn't gone into a Gated Community of the Mind where there was no room for compassion or justice in government or life. His compassion had always been the best part of him, though sometimes his fear fought it, kept it hidden.

"You haven't changed at all," you said. "I was so glad to get your call, to hear you were swinging back through town."

"Swinging?" he echoed, and there it was still, the half-mocking tone in his voice, though you thought the years had watered it down a bit, as they water down all things.

"You don't mean you're . . . staying? Moving back to town?" you managed to ask.

"Well, I *am* heading on to Atlanta tonight for business, like I told you. But I thought I might . . . just see what real estate was doing here, what was available. Just . . . in case." He paused.

"I've put my Chicago place up for sale," he mumbled.

Your eyes met. You wondered if his vulnerable look was affectation. You damned him for his vulnerable look. No, you thought, no, he mustn't do this to you, not before you had your say.

"It's *through the roof,* real estate," you said, throwing your left arm up on the back of the sofa in a proprietary way and sitting back, remembering the light and breezy manner you had selected for tonight to go along with the Armani. "Thinking of . . . investing?" you threw out, and you hoped he didn't hear your gulp. He had a small pimple under his right eye and you remembered, as you always did when you saw him in person, that he was mortal, human, fallible. You loved him more for it. For some reason you recollected a particular Saturday afternoon thirty years ago when the two of you had been playing War with the other neighborhood boys, and the area under his nostrils had been dirty, grimy.

"What?" he asked. Your eyes had betrayed you for one moment.

"Nothing. I was just thinking of something . . . but I'm being wicked rude, I haven't asked you yet if you want anything. What do you want? Have a beer?" and you slid the ice bucket in his direction. He studied the bucket, its contents.

"Okay. Ahh, there's only one there, though," he said, half-laughing, pointing. He still liked to point, apparently.

"I'm having the tonic," you said. "So, how's Chicago?"

"You're having the tonic?" he asked, and he lifted the beer from the bucket, twisted the cap off it, and its "hiss, gush" was a siren to you. "You quit?"

"Why do you sound so surprised?" you asked, and you sat back again and crossed your legs as you brought the bottle to your lips.

"Wow, you . . . well, I don't mean to sound surprised but . . . wow. Sean the wild man? Sean that nobody could tell what to do? The Party Animal? Hmmph. I guess you've changed, huh?"

"Well, I'm sober now. But I think of it . . . I like to think of it as becoming the person I always was, trying to become the best part of myself."

Now for it. You took a deep breath and tried to speak slowly. "But really, I haven't changed at all. I've . . . I think I was always this person, this person you see now—" you vaguely waved not at yourself but at the objects around you—"and I just needed the . . . right circumstances to bring that out in me. You helped me a lot in a way."

He laughed then, a little, but his face jerked back as if he'd been slapped. There was a sadness in his eyes now. You thought the years of corporate consumerist one-upmanship were taking their toll on him.

"Really? Hmmmph. I . . . well. And ahh . . . how have I helped you?"

"Well, as I recall, you . . . you started being a little . . . embarrassed about me, I think. Ashamed of your roots, of our roots. Of where we lived? And you made me see that . . . there was another way to live. Another someone I could be."

Again you vaguely waved at the things in the room.

"Well," he said. He clasped his hands together. His jaw tightened. He looked away first.

"I think . . . embarrassed might be . . . too strong a word," he said lowly.

"Oh, come on, Tim; let's call a spade a spade," you said. "You were embarrassed. The last two years you didn't even . . . you wouldn't even tell people you were from Southie, or that—"

"I just wanted something better, that's all," he sulked. "Is that so wrong? Looks like you did too, huh?"

He looked around the room.

"Well, I guess you were the first one to put that idea into my head." You paused for a minute; something he said had pissed you off. "But . . . something better? Tim, what was better than . . . than what we had? All those years?"

"Sean, I had an opportunity. You know that," he said quietly. He started picking the label off his beer with his thumb. He wouldn't look at you.

"Of course you did. More than, evidently, more than anything you had here." At this point you had to tell yourself to calm down, to keep speaking slowly, casually. You could hear the blood thumping in your ears, it sounded like booted soldiers tramping, tramping.

"Sean, don't. . . . Sean, please don't pretend that things weren't crazy, that you . . . that your drinking and . . . and the other stuff wasn't getting out of control."

"Well, you're right. You're right, Tim. I was . . . an alcoholic. Still am. But a recovering one now."

You pursed your lips and looked up at him.

"But . . . I just . . . I dunno Tim, I always got the feeling . . . I just had the feeling there was more to your leaving than that. I think you were looking for someone with a fancier address than D Street."

He looked down. His beer-bottle peeling was furious now.

"I mean," you went on, "when you started hanging out with all those new South End friends and all and . . . I mean, don't tell me that stuff didn't always turn your head, Tim. The right cars. The right addresses. The right people."

He said nothing, stared down at his shoes.

"So what if they did?" he finally mumbled. "Looks like you've subscribed to the same theory."

He jerked his head again toward this room, the things in this room, this place.

You held his eyes and tried not to smile.

"And I assume you've found what you were looking for?" you asked him. "You've . . . done okay yourself?"

"I've done okay," he said.

"Lost your "dese-and-doze" accent anyway, I see," you said. "Well, whatever, Tim. The bottom line is you left me, took off to Chicago, and . . . well, I guess that was that. Eight years ago? Hard to believe." You paused, took another sip of tonic. "And then when I didn't hear from you . . . and of course I had no way of getting in touch with you . . ."

"You think that was easy?" he asked, and he almost snorted. "You think I didn't pick up the phone a thousand times all these years?"

"Oh? There were—" and you gulped again, couldn't help it "—there were no others? You didn't . . . replace me?" You snorted. "I can't believe that."

Your eyes slammed into his. He folded his arms, put down his beer.

"Well?" you pressed, like a child.

"There were one or two," he said. He took a deep breath and when he lifted those blue eyes up to you they were like lasers. "But there comes a time," he continued, "when you . . . well." He stopped, looked around. Made a point of looking at Mark's picture on the mantel. He picked up his beer again. Gulped it with lowered, restless eyes. "I guess it's a moot point now anyway."

He did this thing with his face, this squirm—he'd always done it when he was mad and he did it again now and you thought you might weep.

"So anyway," he said. He looked around, fixed his eyes again on the picture of Mark on the mantel.

"Is that your . . ."

"That's Mark," you said.

His lower lip stuck out and he folded his hands in front of him, nodded.

"Yeah, we've both done pretty well for ourselves. Mark's a doctor and I own my own business. In fact, I just finished work."

"So this isn't all his?" he said. "You're not his little . . ."

He never finished sentences like that, which always made his inferences darker, more insulting. You felt your face coloring. He set his lips grimly to see that he had scored a direct hit.

But you smiled, fluttered your eyelids, managed to smile and look down and reply casually, "That's just my point. Tim. You just proved what I'm saying. Your assumptions about . . . about this—" (you spread your arms out and nodded toward the room, the things in the room) "—aren't exactly a vote of confidence in my favor, are they? That's what I'm getting at. That's my whole point. I never felt that. . . . Well, I mean I did in the early years . . . but once you met those other friends of yours, once you started going to college, I never felt that just me was enough for you. I had the feeling you were ashamed of me, ashamed of our roots. That you wanted me to become . . . something I wasn't. A person with a pedigree, and things, all kinds of things."

He sulked, when all you wanted was for him to apologize. He glowered. You became bewildered over just which one of his moods made you want him more.

"The thing is," you repeated, "I own my own business now. Mark's a doctor and does quite well, but I've got my own business now and I couldn't take on another client if I wanted to."

He looked up at you from his shoes, nodded. "Well . . . that's good." He folded his hands. He actually cracked his knuckles, and he hadn't done that since one moment before your first touch, when you were both seventeen. "What is it?" he asked. "What's your business?" and now he wasn't even bothering to shield the anger in his eyes, the regret, everything. His right knee started bouncing and the part of you that had planned this evening rejoiced at his acute discomfiture. This wasn't the healthiest part of you, you thought.

You smiled again. "Uhff, please. I just finished work—that's the last thing I want to talk about," you said. "But you sound . . . angry almost. Regretful. You got your wish though, Tim—here I am, no longer the working-class slob. So you got your wish."

"Sean, I—"

"What . . . what made your feelings change for me? From love to shame? What was it, Tim?"

He looked away, crossed his legs, brought the beer halfway to his mouth then brought it down to his lap again.

"Sean, you were. . . . Don't pretend you weren't getting out of control."

"No, I mean, before that. Way before that. Fuckin' . . . the night I went to pick you up at your school and I was early and came up to you and some of your school friends."

"I don't remember that."

"I do. I was cutting across the street and for the first time, when your eyes met mine, they didn't . . . it was like, you weren't happy to see me. In front of your school friends. It just stopped me dead."

He didn't say anything.

"So you see, Tim, maybe it was a good thing that you left me. Left me when I . . . when I . . . begged you to stay."

"You were out of control!" he cried, and you made yourself look disappointed at his emotional display, as if such outbursts were inappropriate to your life now, to the hushed and hushing objects surrounding you at this moment. "When I started *my* business and that night we went out to dinner with my backers—"

"I embarrassed you?"

"Well, Jesus Christ, what do you think? Showing up dressed like that and half in the bag and . . . and then when Dennis had his party . . . "

"It was so important that you make a nice impression on those new best faggy friends of yours from the South End, wasn't it?" you asked. "Where are they now, by the way?" Your breathing was heavy; you lost it for a moment and pointed at him. "You forgot where you came from, Tim. You forgot loyalty. Maybe . . . maybe you feeling ashamed of me had a lot to do with my drin—well, never mind." The blame game, you were playing the blame game and you hadn't done that in years.

There was a sound out of him and you looked up to see what it was. It sounded like a sob, a catching in his throat, but he had dispatched it by the time you looked.

"*Loyalty?*" he said. "Jesus Christ! I just didn't want to spend the rest of my life in your D Street apartment! I was sick of the craziness! I wanted to *do* something with my life! And I wanted *you* to do something with *your life!*"

"Well, I guess you got your wish then, Tim. Looks like we've both done something with our lives. But . . . excuse me, I thought . . . I thought it was *our* D Street apartment. I thought we *were* doing something with our lives. We were . . . we were being together."

This was the crux of it. You fumed, rearranged things on the coffee table. You tried to center yourself, breathed deeply.

You exhaled loudly.

"I forgive you," you said. "I really have. I've forgiven you a long time ago. I just . . . I'm sorry."

You got confused for a minute as to whether you were still playing the game or not. You began to think this wasn't such a good idea, punishing him like this. It wasn't. But your mouth shot off again.

"I mean, what does that mean exactly? Do something with my life? Does that mean buy a certain car or have a certain job or . . . I mean, what does that mean? Why are you ashamed of where you come from?"

He wouldn't look at you after you said that.

You wouldn't look at him. He was holding his beer so tightly you thought the bottle might explode.

But it didn't. His mannerisms, the way he said things, everything, was screaming how sorry he was. The fact that he was here, had sought you out, made the first move—but you wanted him to say it. You wanted to hear it, even though you knew it was impossible for him to say he was wrong; he never could. Even when things had been at their best between the two of you, he could never say those words. There would be flowers from him, there would be tears and hugs, but never could he admit that he was wrong, and that was what you were waiting for. His mouth actually opened, but then he saw how your face was set, and he closed it again.

After that there really was nothing left to say. You looked at the Rolex on your wrist; you had to. He grunted—or was it a groan?— smiled quickly, got up. He shoved his hands deep into his pockets, rattled his change, looked around. He looked brittle then and you almost lost it again. But you didn't, you gathered up the ice bucket, the empty beer and tonic bottles. He went in front of you, held the kitchen door open for you. You couldn't look at the back of him, for fear you'd miss your step.

The two of you walked back out into the hall, to where the foyer and parlor met. Now his face was set.

He turned and walked to the front door. He kept his back to you; he stopped. You thought that if the two of you embraced now, the embrace would never end. But he kept his hands in his pockets as he turned. At last he pulled a hand out, extended it.

"Glad to see you've done so well," he said. "And . . . I really mean this, Sean. I wish . . . you and Mark all the happiness there is in the world."

You laughed then. The clock chimed and you knew you wouldn't have to wait long; Mark and Brad were beyond anal when it came to time and they'd be home any minute.

"Could you just wait here for a minute, Tim?" you said. "Please? I need to do a few things, but hang on. I'll walk out with you; just hang on a minute."

His face shifted a bit.

"Can you do that? Just wait a minute?"

"Okay," he mumbled. He grimaced and looked down at his shoes.

You went into the parlor and pulled open the drawer of the mahogany table. You pulled out the oval-framed picture you had placed there earlier and returned it to the mantel, beside the other picture, its mate. You went upstairs, back to the dressing room, and took off the Armani suit. You wiped it clean as you hung it back up, right where it belonged—you'd seen it there often. You grabbed your dirty clothes from the bottom of the closet. You slipped off the three-hundred dollar shoes in a kind of daze, shoved them back onto the shoe rack. You closed the walk-in closet's door, then opened the third drawer down in the bureau, where you placed the Rolex watch. This is where it was kept. You looked again at its inscription, TO MARK FROM BRAD—HAPPY FIRST ANNIVERSARY.

You opened your old shopping bag and put on your T-shirt, your sweatpants, your white socks—still damp—and your sneakers. An odor of ammonia and floor wax still clung to your shirt.

You went back down to the kitchen and rinsed out the tonic bottle, then the beer bottle. Before you rinsed out the beer bottle you brought it to your lips, inhaled. You closed your eyes and licked the rim of the bottle—not for the alcohol but for the scent of his mouth. You gently slid the bottle into your mouth.

You rinsed out the ice bucket, dried it with a yellow and blue plaid dishcloth, put it back. You opened up the top kitchen drawer beside the refrigerator, and found the check made out to your business in its usual place, the usual amount. You went into the front hall and took out a vacuum cleaner, a pail filled with cleaning liquids, and a mop.

Tim's face was squirming when he saw you.

"Sean, what the hell is going on?" he growled.

Mark and Brad came in just as he asked that question.

"Oh. Hello," Mark said.

"Hey, guys. This is my . . . friend Tim."

"Oh. Hey. Hello, Tim." There were handshakes all around. Tim could barely sputter a polite response.

"The place looks great, Sean, as usual," Mark said. "Thanks. You get your check okay?"

"I did," you said. "Thanks."

Tim turned to you as you picked up the vacuum cleaner, your cleaning supplies, and you knew that he got it now; he knew that you had tricked him. Why did you?

"We're going out again in a minute—can we drop you somewhere?" Brad asked, going through the mail you had piled on the hall desk when you first got here.

You shook your head.

"I'll just cab it," you said. You always took a cab, the last job of the day. "I borrowed a beer and a tonic," you told them.

"Help yourself, you know that," Brad said, not looking up from the mail. He was doing that nose-twitching tic again. You thought of a grain-reaping machine, the way he was sifting through the mail, a mountain of mail. When you went home you never thought of work.

"See you next Thursday, guys," you called as you held open the door. Tim went first.

He didn't have to ask what that was all about as you walked down to the corner in silence, side by side. There was a noise coming out of him again but you couldn't be sure of what it was. You didn't look.

He stopped suddenly. In front of you. You felt sorrowful, now that you'd done it.

"I'm sorry," you said. "I just . . . I wanted you to . . ."

He held his palm up. That was a memory-bash too; he used to do that when he needed a minute.

"No," you said, "no, I need to say this. I just . . . I see that it was a shitty thing for me to do now, but I wanted to show you what it might've been like if I became that person you wanted me to be. Defined by my things. The harmless little consumer."

"I felt so . . . I felt so belittled by you, Tim."

The two of you resumed walking.

You stopped at the corner, at the taxi stand.

"You're right," he said. "It was a shitty thing to do."

The two of you stared at each other.

"I'm not ashamed of who I am anymore," you announced.

You noticed his eyes were red-rimmed. They never looked bluer than when they were red-rimmed, like Japanese Iris they were.

The cabbie recognized you. He got out and opened the trunk of his vehicle, helped you stow your cleaning things.

"D Street, man?" the cabbie asked you.

Tim's head shot up.

"Yeah," you said, climbing into the backseat.

Your eyes held Tim's. You kept the door ajar. You had one foot on the sidewalk still. Tim was standing there alone, on the corner, his eyes rusting wounds, his hands jammed into the pockets of his microfiber pants. Behind him the sky was vermilion, electric.

"Do you want to talk?" you asked him. "I promise I'll be me this time."

AN HOUR LATER in your place, in your apartment, lying on your bed, you looked at your naked body awash in the sodium streetlight, at how the D Street light fell onto the old tattoo on your right delt: IRISH PRIDE, the scroll read, above a Celtic knot, the symbol for eternity. That last part had been Tim's idea, when you both got matching tattoos when you were seventeen. That night you two had made love for the first time. *Jesus,* you thought, *nineteen years ago.* You took out the pieces of that night, you played with them: the flopping and shifting of seventeen-year-old limbs and hands and torsos, the shaking, reaching fingers, had been awkward at first; but the deepest place inside you knew what it was doing—it sang, flowed, gleamed. You swore, still swore, you could see a light coming out of the both of you. He had sobbed in your arms when you finished because the whole world had shattered into a flowering. Right in this apartment, in this very bed. You recalled how this small room had filled up that night with the smell of his hot sneakers, his sweat. Like wet leaves, like a ripe garden, the room had smelled. While he sobbed, in release, in bewilderment, in love, you had traced the outline of his tattoo. Shyly at first, whispering to him over and over that his tears were waterfalls of eternity. It was the one poetic utterance you had ever given vent to. At the time you had thought the phrase was dumb, senseless; but then later you remembered how you had dreamed his blue eyes were waterfalls, and you began to have hope then in the world, in things, began to believe that I had made the world connected. That I wanted people to love one another, love life.

I did. I do.

When you had changed his tears to laughter by and by, he was ravenous, ravenous, and you filled the two of you with blueberry Pop-Tarts. That was his favorite then. You had toasted them out in the kitchen, shouting to him "No peeking, no sniffing"; it was a surprise. You arranged them in the pattern of a wheel on an old tray that had belonged to your grandmother. The tray depicted songbirds of Ireland. The ice-cold glasses of milk you served with them had wobbled as you carried the tray back into the bedroom. The two of you had eaten them at the end of the rumpled bed on your bellies, watching the TV, the blue light washing over his naked body. You couldn't get

over the white silkiness of him. You'd known him all your life, had
seen him every day of your life, and now this. There was the darkness
of his hair, the reddish tan around his neck, and then a plunging into
uninterrupted whiteness to the soles of his feet. His body was a
smooth line that rose and fell and rose and fell and rose and fell. Neither one of you could concentrate; you kept looking at each other and
laughing. It seemed an antidote to everything sorrowful in the world,
having it be okay, allowable, to reach over and stroke the flesh of his
behind.

That was how it was the first night. And so many like it afterward.

THE SHOWER WATER STOPPED and your reverie did as well. He
had come back here with you now, ridden silent in the cab with you.
You had shown him what you had done to the place. You had bought
the other unit upstairs five years ago, had knocked down walls. There
was someone in The Program who crafted handmade furniture, and
you had bought one or two pieces a year. You had covered some of the
walls with old barn board. You had found an old fireplace on the second floor, and had opened it up. Last, you showed him the bedroom.
You had put French doors on the back wall, and it looked out onto the
walled garden now. You had taken out the rusted clothesline, the old
cement patio. There was a tree at the far end and you had draped it
with blue Christmas lights. You turned them on so he could see the
neat rows of beans, the tomato plants humped along the south wall,
the sunflowers lining the north wall like nodding sentries. There was a
statue of an old saint under the tree; you'd found it in a junkyard. You
told him how you put birdseed on the shoulders of the saint and that
the birds came for it every day.

After the tour he asked if he could use the bathroom, freshen up after his flight. Otherwise you hadn't really spoken. The two of you had
stared straight ahead on the cab ride home.

Once he was in the bathroom you had vacillated, but then finally
you stripped. You were lying on the bed now, naked. You thought if
he came out of the bathroom fully dressed and ready to leave you
might not survive the humiliation.

Yes, you would. There was a meeting at 7:30 and you would go to the meeting if worse came to worst. You'd been through too much. To calm yourself you murmured a favorite old song of your grandmother's, a love song. Your grandfather had wooed her with it. Why you thought of that now, you didn't know at first:

> No matter I've waited a very long time
> To ask you if you could but spare me some time

But you couldn't recall the tune really and you kept getting it confused with "There Is a Balm in Gilead," which you had both sung in the third grade for the May procession.

The bathroom door opened. He turned the light off behind him. A puff of Ivory soap scent floated into the bedroom before he did. He was still drying off his backside with the white towel as he stepped into the hall. He was being as boldly tentative as yourself. Other than that, he was naked. Your eyes, your jaw, tightened with heat. Again, you understood his pride. Or was it fear?

When he saw you like that on the bed, he froze. Your hands were behind your head to keep them from trembling. You had draped the edge of the comforter over your groin to hide the ridiculousness of your tumescence in case he should emerge dressed.

By the sodium streetlight you could see his jaw tighten, his head turn away. A sob came out of his mouth. He disguised it with a cough.

You rose from the bed. At first you didn't go to him; you lit candles instead. You had set out a flock of candles on the night tables, on the dresser by the wall. The room warbled in the light. You could feel his eyes on you.

You walked over to him. You looked at each other. The years apart fell away like parched cocoons; you could almost hear the sifting of them as they fell and blew off. You touched him on his arm, traced your finger down to his fingers. He closed his eyes, his mouth fell open. The groan out of him was like scorched eiderdown, soft, yet burning. You took him in your arms. His towel fell to the floor. He really lost it then, convulsions running through him.

"Shhhh, shhhh," you soothed him, your hands like devouring eyes on the back of him. "Welcome home, Timmy," you said. "Welcome home."

It wasn't the poetry you wanted, but it would do.

You're Always Happy When You're Rich

anny padded down for breakfast on the May morning of his nineteenth birthday, and found his mother bustling around in the kitchen, burning things. Inadequate blocks of sun rested on the kitchen floor, too small to warm or really lighten.

"Hi. How come you're home?" Danny rumpled his dark bed-messed hair and yawned. He stood uncertainly in the middle of the room, wearing the white T-shirt and plaid boxers he'd worn to bed the night before.

"I'm going in a little late," Mrs. Sullivan clucked. She hustled over to Danny and kissed his cheek. "And I'll tell you why: Happy birthday, honey! I'm making you *French toast!*" She was wearing a white cotton dress with small bunches of scarlet roses on it, one she wore only in summer. The dress was hopeful and made Danny think there might still be Possibilities.

Mrs. Sullivan seemed happily oblivious to the smoke puffing from an aluminum frying pan on the back of the stove. She smiled and said, "Go into the parlor for a little while and I'll call you when it's done."

Danny headed back upstairs to the bedroom he shared with his brother, George. He pulled on navy blue nylon sweatpants with orange stripes running down the sides. When he returned downstairs, he stopped at the open front door in the parlor and stood in the sunlight. He looked out through the glass storm door that would never shut tight. The view was the same as always. The jammed triple-deckers right across the street, the continuous lines of parked cars, the sky a crowded-out afterthought and not a tree in sight. For the first time Danny gave thought to the worry that had been licking at him for the past year—what if he got stuck here for life?

He shook the thought away and touched the storm door for luck. He pushed it open and leaned his head out, breathing deeply. The air was warm with sun and there was no hint yet of the sea's tang, nor the city's pollution—two more hopeful signs. This is how the air must smell everywhere else, Danny thought. Fresh and clear and full of Possibilities.

"Okay, honey," Mrs. Sullivan called.

Danny slid a smile on his face and strode out to the kitchen. Mrs. Sullivan had shoved the old mail and newspapers off to one side of the round tippy kitchen table, and set a place for Danny. He saw a plate stacked high with French toast swimming in Vermont Maid syrup to which, Danny knew, his mother had added water so there would be enough. At the top of his plate sat a cracked glass with a purple lilac in it. The buds hadn't quite opened yet. Danny could smell only the very well-done French toast and his mother's perfume, the one she wore every day to work.

Resting next to his plate was an unopened letter addressed to him. He froze. His heart felt like it was spinning when he read the return address, that of a college twenty miles south of Boston.

"It came yesterday, honey, but I saved it for this morning, for your birthday," Mrs. Sullivan explained, leaning against the salt-and-pepper kitchen countertop, her small pink hands clasped tightly across her stomach. She cleared her throat and sang, "I have a good feeling about this one!"

My last chance, Danny thought.

He plunked down in the creaky wooden chair and stabbed his fork into the French toast. He shoved a stack of four small drippy pieces into his mouth. His mother had cut it up for him too.

"It's thicker," she said, rushing over to the table and snatching the letter. She waved it in front of Danny's face. "It's thicker than the other letters." She put it back down on the table in front of Danny.

Right after New Year's Danny had applied to seven colleges. Six of those had rejected him.

Danny wished he'd brought the mail in himself yesterday, but he'd been working on a design upstairs in his bedroom and the day had run away from him. He wished it right now almost as powerfully as he wished he'd get into this school. His stomach squirmed with this wish.

"Well?" Mrs. Sullivan chirped, folding her hands again and working them together.

Danny looked at his mother. She was smiling but her gray eyes were large and liquidy with worry. He smiled weakly. He picked up the letter. It *was* heavier. He saw himself walking beneath the September shade of large sighing trees, textbooks under his arm, an ivy-covered building in the distance. He saw too what he'd be wearing. Off-white khakis, a green-and-white plaid button-down shirt with the cuffs rolled halfway up his forearms, a baseball cap the same color as his pants, new dark-brown hiking boots. There wouldn't be anyone walking with him, not yet; but in his head he'd be entertaining the possibility that soon there would be—

"Can I have some juice, Ma, please?" Danny mumbled. He couldn't swallow the syrupy mass with the clutch in his throat.

In a spurt, juice was in front of him. He gulped half the glass, avoiding his mother's eyes.

He opened the envelope and pulled the letter out. It was folded in thirds. There was some kind of enclosure inside the letter, a thick, hot-pink card that skidded onto the table, face up. It was this college's football schedule for the upcoming fall season, and some information on homecoming week. Danny's lips pulled together. His eyes narrowed and he grew a little dizzy.

"I think I might be in," he half-roared.

"Oh, God, I knew it, *knew* it!" Mrs. Sullivan cried, bringing one hand to her mouth.

"Wait," Danny said, holding up his finger.

He flipped open the letter with a loud flick of his index finger.

Dear Mr. Sullivan,
The Board of Admissions would like to thank you for applying to our college.

Danny's breath caught—they always thanked you first when they rejected you. Thanks but no thanks.

He looked up at his mother. She was frozen, leaning forward like she might topple, her eyes more anxious than Danny's.

She stared at Danny's face like it was her last meal. "Not . . . not bad news?" she asked.

Danny's eyes fell to the letter again.

> After careful consideration of your application and records, the Board of Admissions regrets that we cannot offer you a seat in the upcoming fall semester at this time. We do wish you every success in your upcoming academic career, and we thank you again for considering our institution.

Danny wished the letter went on so he could keep reading, reading and reading and reading, anything to avoid his mother's eyes. He lingered over the sky blue signature—*D. Kerwin MacDonald, Director of Admissions,* and the small PRINTED ON RECYCLED PAPER written around an image of a green tree at the bottom of the page.

He heard the click of his mother's lighter as she lit up a cigarette, heard her waving her arms as she flailed the exhaled smoke away from her. He could taste his disappointment, his tongue curled with its acidity. He felt his cheeks redden with humiliation: to have his failure observed by his mother, by anyone. It would have been the same with a stranger from the street, called in as a witness.

"Dan-ny! Dan-ny! Dan-ny!" his entire eighth-grade phys ed class had chanted when he'd tripped running into the gym—over nothing, over himself—and sprawled out on the waxed wood floor. He could hear them again in his head now, out in the street, upstairs in the hall, inside the oven—

He carefully folded the letter back into thirds, placing the pink football schedule inside. Then he ripped it up.

"Danny!" his mother wailed, her voice breaking.

"It's okay," Danny heard himself say. His voice sounded dead. He looked down at the congealing French toast, the flowery pattern of the chipped plate.

"What about UMass honey? They'll take anyb—I mean, you could *start* there, and with your brains transfer . . . transfer *anywhere.*"

"It's too late," Danny mumbled.

"Too late? What do you mean, too late? For Chris'sake, it's only May. How can it be—"

"I called them last week just in case," Danny said. He pushed the French toast away. "The deadline was two weeks ago for fall . . . admissions."

"Jesus Christ! Don't these people know about the busing? Don't they know what *happened* to the schools around here?"

They didn't know, Danny knew, or if they did, they didn't care. The forced busing to achieve racial integration had begun Danny's freshman year. Riots, helicopters overhead, the National Guard and baton-wielding tactical police, to say nothing of stone- and bottle-throwing parents, had prevented Danny and his brother from going to school across town more than three days the first two quarters. The school administration had been notified by the courts that absenteeism by white students was just a form of boycott in an attempt to disrupt justice, and that such students, if they didn't show up, would be failed. In everything.

Sophomore year had been almost as bad.

They didn't have the money for private schools. Mrs. Sullivan would have put the house up for sale to afford that expense—if she owned it. She had said that twenty times a day those two years. *If I owned this house, kids—*

Danny's brother, George, had dropped out, but was lucky enough to get on part-time with the gas company when he was sixteen. Now twenty-one, he was full-time and "set for life," as he told Danny and his mother. He was saving money and dating a teacher that he'd probably marry.

Danny thought he'd rather die than work for the gas company for the rest of his life.

By junior year things had calmed down a bit, though the schools— without books for many of the students, and with fights every day— were in little danger of turning out Rhodes scholars. Unlike students in the snow-white suburbs west of Boston—where lived the judges and legislators and newspaper owners who were determined that busing, in Boston, *would* be implemented no matter the cost—it was difficult to learn anything when each day was a variation on a theme of chaos.

But junior year also had seen the rotten blossoming of That Other Thing, the thing that ate at Danny night and day.

The only relief had been his design work, the plans he drew for houses and buildings far from urban noise and every kind of confusion.

"Well . . . well then, next year, honey," Mrs. Sullivan said. "Next year, that's all." Her face puckered as she sucked on her cigarette.

"Yeah," Danny mumbled. He looked up at his mother and smiled. "Yeah. Next year. You better go, Ma."

"I know, honey. Call me if you need to talk. Are you all right?" She leaned over and kissed her son on the cheek.

"Yeah, I'm fine. Fine."

"Okay, well . . . well, happy birthday, sweetheart." She smiled, and turned and put her cigarette out in a half-full cup of cold coffee in the sink. Then she grabbed her oversized pocketbook and trooped out the back door.

"Yeah," Danny whispered. "Happy fucking birthday."

And Ma had had a *good feeling about this one.* Danny snorted. He appreciated her support, in *everything*—but her problem was she couldn't tell the difference between a good feeling and a wish. When Dad had left after an especially loud midnight fight, she'd told Danny and George he'd be back in a month, that he just needed some space. That was six years ago. Since then she'd redoubled her concern for her two boys, now that the hovering she lavished on her husband was in reserve.

You're so smart, Danny—you can be anything you want, she'd always tell him. *You'll be a fantastic architect.* Now, sitting at the quiet kitchen table, he was trying to remember why he'd ever believed her. He was a loser. His mother was just too wonderfully loyal to see this.

He'd always liked building things. As a child he delighted in taking a pile of toy blocks or sticks and making something out of nothing. He and George would dump out a clattering barrel of Tinker Toys or Lincoln Logs onto the parlor rug. George would get bored after fifteen minutes, but never Danny. When he was eleven, he built a flying saucer that twirled around while he held it, and when he sent the plans to Tinker Toys, they'd reprinted them in their instruction booklet and sent him a check for twenty-five dollars.

He'd started designing houses when he was twelve. When he was thirteen he moved inside these houses, planning where each room would be and how it would flow into the next one. He would assign furniture for each room, and then, finally, think about the life he might lead in these rooms among this furniture when he became a man, passing from room to quiet sunny room. The rooms would be fragrant with the smell of nothing.

With each house he'd design, Danny would spend the most time on the master bedroom. Usually it was L-shaped and the smaller wing contained the dressing area. He had seen this in a *House Plans Magazine* he'd once bought with his allowance. *Dressing area.* It sounded private, mysterious—almost sacred. Quickly this became his favorite space to envision and design. Quiet with sun, Danny always pictured it. A view of the sky through the large windows and skylight. The sky would always be the color of a particular cerulean china cup his grandmother owned. A soft wall-to-wall carpet that Danny's bare feet would fall into. A mirrored wall to watch himself dress.

He could see himself in this room, see how he'd look as a man. Bigger, more polished. A registered architect by then. Quietly putting on a suit in the morning—quiet with the confidence and inner strength that came with being a man, as opposed to his quietness now, born of grief and bewilderment. Putting on a dark suit in the morning. Not too early—about the time when shafts of light would spill across the room and fall, tenderly, like music, from the skylights.

He never pictured the dressing area at the end of the day, never at night. He didn't dare to think of whom he might share this space with. He'd see only himself, in the mornings, watching himself getting dressed after a shower. It was too much to hope for anything else. If he could make it to that master bedroom, if he could find himself standing barefoot on the sun-warmed rug in the dressing area—if he could make it that far from here, everything else he wanted and needed would fall into place. He knew this.

"IT'S ONLY A YEAR," George said quietly when he came home from the gas company at 3:35 p.m. It took George five minutes to walk home from work and he was never late. He sat down on his twin bed across from Danny's and took off his black work boots and thick pilly white socks, peeled off his blue chinos and bright orange gas company T-shirt.

They looked like twins despite the three-year age difference. For many years, especially after their father left when they would sleep in the same bed for comfort, they had thought of themselves as one person. Two years ago—when George went full-time and met Mary, the schoolteacher—George had grown a goatee to signify, Danny knew, that they were separate people. Still brothers but separate now.

"I know, but a whole year," Danny had mumbled, looking up from his bed, where he'd spent the day masturbating with joyless eagerness. Plus, UMass Boston, an urban campus, had no large trees, no ivy-covered halls, but instead modern, mostly windowless box buildings designed by architects with unpronounceable names, whose own children would never go to such a place. By its appearance it could just as easily be a jail, or an overly swollen medical building on Route 1. And Danny could see UMass from down at the beach; it was right across the harbor. Too close. Much too close.

"You can have anything you want if you work hard enough for it," George said, stretching out. In another minute he was sleeping, breathing lightly, his face and one knee turned away from the lean plane of his muscled body.

Danny raised his head and watched his brother's breathing. He envied George's fulfillment of his destiny, so soon in life. George was smart, too smart for the gas company, and he knew it. But he was set for life now. George gave them eight hours a day. In return they gave him a good paycheck, security for life, and zero stress, and he was home every day by 3:35 to nap. Then out each night with Mary, or off to a Red Sox game with friends exactly like himself. He'd marry Mary soon and buy a house on the West Side, upgrading every few years and hop-scotching closer and closer to the East Side until they were right on the water, the South Boston equivalent to Nirvana.

Danny wished that such a life, for him, would be anything other than a death sentence to his soul. That would make it so much easier. Instead he wanted to be an architect.

Or nothing at all.

HE CALLED MR. PALMER that night.

"I can work full-time this summer," Danny told his answering machine, "and ah . . . into the fall too." His eyes on the future, Danny had planned on working only until mid-August, twenty hours a week. He needed time to dream of the tree-covered campus he'd be going to. But that, of course, had changed now. Mr. Palmer had inherited a painting company from his father. When the old man ran it, it was called Ask Mr. Palmer!, and his truck would be seen all over South Boston, with smaller words above the company's name asking *WHAT COLOR SHOULD I PAINT MY HOUSE? WHO HAS THE BEST PRICE IN TOWN? WHO'S FULLY INSURED?* Now that his son was in charge, the company name had been shortened to Palmer Painting, and they focused exclusively on the East Side, on the grand old homes that were being snapped up for almost a million dollars and, after that, being totally rehabbed. "New People," his mother called them, nonnative professionals whom she blamed for driving up her rent. "It's like an invading army," she'd say, shaking her head, whenever she spotted a Volvo wagon or BMW on the street.

Mr. Palmer called back later that night and asked Danny to start the next day.

"The market's going crazy," he said. "We'll have three or four jobs going at once all summer long." Danny could see in his mind Mr. Palmer's nervous tic, the twitching of the thin lips as they added up his growing profits.

"Okay," Danny sighed. Mr. Palmer didn't ask him, "What about college?" It wasn't out of lack of courtesy, Danny knew; he just hadn't remembered.

The crew was divided into scrapers, painters, and detailers. The detailers were the skilled people who painted scrolls, filigrees, grapevine motifs on lintels. Danny was a scraper. Danny felt he could do the de-

tailers' work better than they did, but he never said anything to con-
tradict the young Mr. Palmer's assumption that a native kid Danny's
age could do nothing better than scrape in the sun all day. Danny
liked the scraping's mindlessness, the way it left room in his brain for
his dreams, for his master bedrooms and dressing areas.

This summer, Mr. Palmer told him the next day, Danny would be
working mostly on his own. The crew was spread out all over the East
Side on different jobs, he said, and he urged Danny to go as fast as he
could while remaining as painstaking as he had been the summer before.

"Now, don't let this responsibility go to your head," Mr. Palmer
said, dropping Danny off at a massive hundred-year-old Philadelphia-
style duplex on O Street.

Danny turned as he hopped out of the truck to see if Mr. Palmer
was joking, but his boss was staring straight ahead, twitching like
crazy as his beeper went off again.

"I think I can handle it," Danny said.

MAY SLID INTO June and the weather grew hot. Danny followed
the sun—or rather, the shade—around the houses he scraped to pro-
tect his whiteness from the scalding he'd given it last year, when he
first started this job. The afternoons were treacherous, for the sea
breeze would kick in around 2:00, keeping him deceptively cool, and
he wouldn't know he'd been burned until he got out of the shower
that night and turned purple. The others on the crew referred to
Danny as The Mummy, for the light-colored clothes he'd swaddle
himself in each day. One more reason he preferred working alone.

On the seventeenth of June, Mr. Palmer dropped him off at a
three-story brick house on East Broadway, one block from City Point
and the ocean. Ragged blue tarps and piles of scrapwood scattered
around the small front yard spoke of extensive recent renovations and
deep pockets. Dry-looking hydrangea bushes shoveled purple and
blue color into the otherwise drab side yard.

"There's forty-five windows in this place," Mr. Palmer told him,
ticcing madly as his cell phone birdcalled away. "Fifteen on each floor.

They're all wood and gotta be scraped clean, real clean." Danny knew "real clean" meant Mr. Palmer was almost extorting the clients. "But there's some really nice detail on the front casements, so you'll have to use sandpaper on those." Mr. Palmer paused to answer his cell phone, but was too late. He turned back to Danny. "Listen to me: this guy's an architect so he *will* notice if any of the detail's missing. The ladders and staging are on the side, like always."

Danny felt a tightening in his throat as Mr. Palmer drove his truck away.

An architect.

It had never occurred to Danny, in his wildest imaginings, that an architect would choose to live in South Boston. But of course South Boston was changing, especially on the East Side, filling up with the new people. If they hadn't grown up here, of course architects would want to live here, in their million-dollar, totally rehabbed homes, five minutes to downtown and a view of the ocean from the top floors . . .

He stared stupidly at the building like he'd never done this before. The morning was still blue-ocean cool but his hands were wet with sweat. He wiped them on his white painter's pants and noticed peripherally the changes these people had already made: the bronze pediment over the door, the antique-brick front walk, the brass lanterns on either side of the double Dorchester doors. The morning sun sauntered into the first floor's large front windows, walking across lustrous hardwood floors and a large Oriental rug with a towering floor plant on it, some kind of palm tree. Danny's breath was coming in jags. His head down, he crossed the street and hustled a block away so he could walk back to the house, slowly, looking at it from a distance, appraising it. As he walked he half closed his eyes, picturing himself in a suit, a leather bag large enough for his renderings slung over his shoulders, coming home. Like the other new people he'd seen around town, he would avoid eye contact with the locals and pick up trash he found blowing in front of his house. That's how everyone could always tell.

It was half an hour before he could bring himself to begin.

DANNY ALWAYS STARTED on the west side of buildings because they were drippy with shade in the mornings. He hoisted up the tallest of the three aluminum ladders, extended it, then shoved it against the house. He almost slipped halfway up.

"Concentrate," he told himself. His heart was racing. He took a few deep breaths, then continued climbing.

When he came to the third-floor window he realized he'd forgotten the scraper, wire brush, and sandpaper. He climbed down and went up again, slowing at the second floor as movement through a window drew his eye. A swiftly moving woman gibbering on a small phone passed by the window. Her dark pageboy-styled hair swung rapidly as she crossed the room. She was dressed nicely but stiffly, Danny thought. She looked about thirtyish. She turned as Danny stopped. Their eyes met for a second and he could hear the woman's voice pause. Danny resumed climbing as she approached the window, her dark brows frowning. Through the slightly opened window Danny heard the woman's footfalls stop. Then he heard the blind come down hard, and the click of the lock after she closed the window.

Back at the third floor, Danny saw through the window the largest room he'd ever seen, except for the gym and auditorium at his old high school. It appeared the entire third floor was one vast room. Newly installed metal beams ran left to right, holding up a gleaming white plaster ceiling. The hardwood floors here shone even more brilliantly than the first floor's, as the sun was flooding unobstructed into the room. Through the luminescent windows across the room, the pale-blue ocean shimmered two blocks away. The walls were painted a deep blue, with arctic-white trim. In the middle of the room sat a vast metal drafting table. It was the room's only piece of furniture.

"Hello? Can I help you?"

Danny jumped and grabbed onto the edges of the reverberating ladder. He looked down carefully. The woman was on the ground beneath him, still on the phone but holding it to her breast with her thin, tan arms folded.

"Uh, I'm the ahh—"

"Oh. Oh, you're one of the painters, aren't you," she said rather than asked, putting one hand on her head as if she'd just remembered this. She rolled her eyes and groaned as if she felt overwhelmed. She lifted up the phone and said, "Hi, Valerie; thanks for holding. No, it's just one of the painters. I forgot they were starting today. . . . No, no, no, I need ten thousand units in Chicago by Monday. *Monday, Valerie . . .*" Her voice trailed off as she vanished around the corner, picking her way carefully around the scattered scrapwood. In a moment Danny heard the heavy front door close and click. Solidly, like a bank vault.

Danny looked back into the third floor.

This must be his studio. The table looked to be made out of aluminum and it shone, blindingly, in the sun. Danny thought it looked like an altar. It was at least ten feet long and five feet wide, and was supported by eight aluminum struts that curved out halfway down to the floor, mimicking human legs. There were tubes and large rolls of papers on the table. Danny squinted and saw more: compasses and slide rulers, thin pencils and pens scattered here and there. A model of a modern-looking building rose from one end of the table. A computer, all of its components black, sat at the other end. There was a funny-looking black leather chair facing the computer.

Danny realized his mouth was open and he shut it abruptly.

He began scraping the flaky wood around the window. The chips sifted into the air. The ones that didn't fly into Danny's auburn hair or onto his red-haired forearms helicoptered downward, spiraling. He was thinking he had never designed—how could he have forgotten this?—but he'd never designed a workspace for himself in any of the houses he'd created. Entry halls, foyers, balconies, kitchens, libraries, dining rooms and, especially, master bedrooms and dressing areas—but never a workspace, an office.

He began to think he was a fraud; that his mind, whatever atom of talent he might have, was not large enough to create a space as big, or costly, as the one he looked at now.

Right before 11:00 Danny again heard the front door close ponderously. Out of the corner of his eye he saw the woman clicking briskly down the sidewalk, a black kid-leather briefcase slung over the shoulder of her navy blazer. The points of her swinging pageboy seemed to cut the air before her. She was still talking on her tiny cell phone. She passed the house, and Danny turned to watch her climb up into a pale-green Range Rover with a circular sticker on the rear bumper that said ACK. This phrase seemed as indecipherable to Danny as the knowledge one would need to have such a house, such a workspace, such a life.

It was not a life one got after attending UMass Boston.

By lunchtime, Danny felt small, nonexistent—light, as if the sea breeze might pick him up at any moment and blow him over to UMass; or possibly back home, to his and George's tiny attic bedroom with the flimsy plywood paneling.

His shoulders stooped, he walked the one block up to McGillicuddy's Spa. Bells jingled as Danny walked in. The place smelled like newspapers and cold cuts. Billy McGillicuddy was working the lunch counter at his parents' place. He and George had played baseball together. Old Massachusetts license plates lined the wall behind him, going back to 1922.

"You been outta town, Danny?" Billy asked, putting down a book he was reading called *Now It Can Be Told*. He wiped his hands on his white apron and shook Danny's hand over the counter. For a second Danny forget his smallness and became lost in the soft blue of Billy's eyes, the sweetness of his smile. He looked different than Danny remembered him.

"Ahh . . . naw. I just . . . I've been painting."

"Oh, cool. For who?"

"Mr. Palmer."

"Ask Mr. Palmer!" Billy grinned. "That'll keep you outta trouble. So, how's Georgie Boy doing? Still with the gas company?"

"Oh, yeah. He's doing good."

"And how about you? How are you doin'?"

"Ahh . . ." Danny felt himself reddening. The more he tried to think of a routine answer, the more tangled his mouth became.

"I thought you were Georgie when you first walked in," Billy said, generously extracting Danny from the mire of his embarrassment.

"Ahh . . . Georgie's got the goatee," Danny said, touching his own smooth chin.

"Well, your eyes are different too," Billy said. His eyes lingered on Danny's. Danny reddened further.

"Stop flirting with the customers!" Danny heard. Aghast, he turned and saw Billy's father, the large Mr. McGillicuddy, sitting low behind the cash register eating a reeking hot-pastrami sandwich. The corners of his mouth were yellow.

"Just being friendly, Dad!" Billy called across the small store, laughing. "I know that's hard for you, but it's a good idea when you deal with the public."

"Friendly, my ass!" Mr. McGillicuddy mumbled through a mouthful of yellow-and-pink food. He turned to Danny. "He flirts with them all, old and young, boys and girls. He'd flirt at his mother's wake."

"So what can I get you, Danny?" Billy asked, scratching his left ear but still smiling.

Danny scanned the menu, written with plastic red letters on a white board hanging from the ceiling behind Billy. He knew his face was as scarlet as the letters. He was looking for something the New People might eat, but could find nothing other than the usual meatball subs and cold-cut sandwiches.

"Ahh . . . lemme have a turkey on rye, a little mayo . . . and lots of black pepper and onions," Danny said, staring at the floor. "Please."

"How's your mother?" Mr. McGillicuddy called.

"Fine, fine," Danny said. Then he blurted out, too loudly, "Fine, thanks."

"And where you working today?"

Danny snagged a small bag of Boyd's potato chips (they had a drawing of a chef winking and making the okay sign) from the metal tree stand beside him and turned around. "Ahh—right down the street," he answered. He pointed. "Right down on the corner."

"Oh. Mary Shea's old place, the Lord be good to 'er," Mr. McGillicuddy nodded. His eyes expanded. "You know her kids got nine hundred-thousand dollars for that place last fall?"

"Wow," Danny murmured, feeling small again. Such a sum seemed like money in a cartoon, a towering pile vanishing into a dizzy, misty height.

"Mary paid twelve-five for it back in the fifties. I remember the day they all moved in," Mr. McGillicuddy went on. He took another boa bite from his sandwich. "Mary and her kids on the first floor, her sister's family on the second, their mother up on the third." He paused and swallowed, then leaned his heavy arms on the top of the cash register, which shifted under the weight. Winning scratch tickets taped to the front of the register jiggled. "Now, her mother was a queer bird. Would never eat in front of anyone. All her life, Mary said."

"A problem my father can't relate to," Billy called from behind the counter.

"Hey, Wise Guy, I'm the comedian today, remember?" Mr. McGillicuddy laughed. He turned back to Danny. "They say they turned the whole goddamn place into a single family," he murmured. "Spent as much as they paid for the place redoing the whole friggin' thing." He paused and shook his head. "All that space for two people—can you imagine? And there were twenty-five in there years ago, and nobody never complained."

"Ahh . . . yeah," Danny answered. A shiver went down his spine and settled in his testicles. He grew bold. "Do you ahh . . . know them at all?"

"What *them?*" Mr. McGillicuddy asked, tossing his head toward the ocean. He laughed. "She came in here once looking for *lah-tay,* if you don't mind. Seemed *offended* that we didn't have it. I told her 'Dear, I'll give you ten bucks if you can find *lah-tay* between here and the Broadway Bridge.' She seemed a little uppity, like the rest of 'em. She bought *The New York Times* on her way out. I said, 'All set for scratch tickets today, dear?'" Mr. McGillicuddy chuckled, his belly shaking beneath his white apron.

"Dad has a flair for chasing new customers away," Billy said dryly.

"And this one got on the phone and ordered a latte machine that afternoon!" Mr. McGillicuddy cried, pointing a plump outraged finger at his son.

"Wait'll I'm running this place, Dad," Billy went on. "Gonna be Yuppie Heaven."

"Jesus wept, don't tell me that!" Mr. McGillicuddy roared. "I'll never retire!" He turned back to Danny but his eyes were laughing.

"*He* seems like a nice enough guy. An architect, somebody said.
Young guy. Comes in for the paper once in a while. Friendly. But still
curious when he's in here, like he's visiting the zoo. I think he travels a
lot for work." Mr. McGillicuddy paused. "Must be *made* o' money."

"Like you'll be, Dad, if you sell the house," Billy joked as he put the
finishing touches on Danny's sandwich.

"And I will, too!" Mr. McGillicuddy roared. "Gonna sell it and
spend it all so the seven of yous won't be fighting over it at my wake!"

"She's gone to Nantucket for the summer," Billy said, handing
Danny his waxed paper–wrapped sandwich. "Right?"

"Ahh . . . I don't know. I saw her this morning," Danny said.

"Maybe just back for the day. Hi-o Higgins did some of the
contractin' inside a few months ago, and he told me she 'summers' in
Nantucket. That's what she told him." Billy chuckled.

"Well, la-dee-da for her," Mr. McGillicuddy boomed. "If someone
told all them phonies that Revere Beach was the new place to go,
they'd swarm up there and settle right in with the guineas. Don't tell
me they wouldn't!"

Billy rolled his eyes. "Daaad," he moaned, half-laughing.

"What, what?" he said, giving Danny his change for a five, "I only
speak the truth! Everyone else thinks this stuff, but I have the balls to
say it!" He turned and winked at Danny. "Hey, what'd you think o'
that trade?"

"Uh . . . trade?"

"The big Sox trade! You didn't hear?" Mr. McGillicuddy's bushy
eyebrows lowered and he leaned into Danny, scrutinizing. It was ob-
vious that Danny hadn't heard, or hadn't cared if he had.

"*Dan-ny! Dan-ny! Dan-ny!*" played in his head as he hurried out the
door.

"See ya later, Danny Boy," he heard Billy call, as the door tinkled
shut behind him.

THE WOMAN RETURNED to the house around 3:30. Danny turned
as if on cue and saw the Range Rover slide up to the curb. She said
nothing as she passed into the house, a matte-gray department store

shopping bag swinging from each hand. Ten minutes later Danny heard urgent footsteps and noise from down on the second floor as he scraped a third-floor window. He tried not to notice a few minutes later when the woman suddenly appeared in the room before him, but their eyes met again. They both looked away instantly. The woman, now in white khaki shorts and a yellow blouse, began closing and locking windows. Danny kept his eye on the casement frame in front of him as she closed the window he was working on. Then she left the room.

Fifteen minutes later she returned to her car and began heaving things into its gaping back. She started up the engine and pulled out into the street. Danny heard the car pause but didn't turn. Then she beeped; Danny knew she was trying to get his attention but still he didn't turn.

"Excuse me," she called, her voice dipped in annoyance.

Danny turned. The woman was leaning way over in her seat, the front passenger window halfway down to keep in the frosty air-conditioning.

"Where's your boss?"

"He's getting supplies," Danny called down. This was the response Mr. Palmer told him to give should a client ever ask for his whereabouts.

"Well, tell him he needs to call me," the woman said behind her sunglasses. Her voice was nasally and tight. "On my cell phone. I won't be back for a month or two." She paused and tilted her head, the points of her hair swinging down like scythes. "Can you do that?"

"Yes," Danny said.

The woman stared at Danny for a moment longer, then she disappeared as the reflective window eased up with an almost apologetic quietness. As the woman drove off Danny wondered what would make her happy, if all of this didn't. It didn't equate; his mind wouldn't accept it. *She must be happy. She's just having a bad day; maybe she's missing her husband. You're always happy when you've made it, when you're rich—*

MR. PALMER CAME BY at a quarter to five, his usual time. His face-twitching doubled when Danny told him "the lady here wants you to call her." His mouth had been open to speak when Danny turned to see him, but his words were forgotten as he rushed back to his truck to make the call. Ten minutes later he reappeared, seemingly relieved.

"How many you do today?" he asked, rubbing his hands together. Danny was just coming down the ladder.

"One," Danny said. Mr. Palmer said nothing. Danny reached for the ladder.

"Leave it up," he said. "I'll check it out. Foot me now, will ya?"

Danny pressed his feet against the bottom of the ladder as Mr. Palmer ascended carefully. The ladder jiggled under his weight. Danny lifted his head and watched his progress. All he could see was Mr. Palmer's legs and buttocks, as if Mr. Palmer were just an ass, carried about on a pair of legs. Danny smiled and reminded himself to tell George about this when he got home. But by then George would be out, and it wouldn't seem funny later.

"It looks good, real good," Mr. Palmer said when he came down. "It's taking a long time though, huh?"

"It is," Danny said, washing his hands at the house's ancient outdoor spigot.

"Well . . ." Mr. Palmer said. He scratched his head. "Just do the best you can. Maybe it'll go a little faster once you get the hang of it."

"Maybe," Danny said.

"Fuck it. She's gone for the rest of the summer anyway, and I think whenever he comes home from traveling he'll go right down there too. So as long as we have most of the job done by then . . ." His voice trailed off as he walked back to his truck.

DANNY SETTLED INTO a bit of a routine, as he did with every job. He brought his lunch every day to avoid further embarrassing conversations at McGillicuddy's, though once or twice Billy McGillicuddy drove by honking and waving. Danny started at 8:00 now, took his lunch from 11:30 to 12:30, then packed up at 3:45. George would be napping by the time he got home. Danny would shower, nap, get up around 8:00, eat the dinner his mother had saved for him, then wander down to the beach or just do design work until about midnight. He wasn't sleeping well. Lying in bed at night, he felt utterly alone and hopeless.

He finished the six windows on the west side of the third floor at the end of his first week. The following Monday he started the front side of the third floor. He slept especially poorly Sunday night, thinking about how the design room, as he called it, would look from this new angle. After lunch on Wednesday afternoon, he moved his ladder over to the third front-facing window. He had finished cleaning the casement with the wire brush when he noticed the window. The blind was drawn but the window was open about an inch. He leaned his head in and sniffed. A chilly smell of newness wafted out to him, a new-house aroma of freshly installed floors and rugs, new furniture—it was the smell of Possibilities. Danny pressed his nose against the screen as he inhaled deeply. To his shock, the screen nudged forward and slipped from its track. He set it to rights again, but couldn't get it down all the way; he was on the wrong side of the window.

Then he froze.

He turned around slowly, looking. The maple behind him—there were plenty of street trees on the East Side—screened him from every direction except for one house across the street at an angle, McGillicuddy's Spa at the other angle, and the sidewalk directly below him. *Don't do it!* a voice inside him shrieked, but something stronger made Danny lift up the screen halfway, then reach in and slide up the window. Before he knew fully what he was doing he was inside the third floor, as shocked and breathless as if he had passed through a mirror. For a minute, two minutes, he could only stand motionless as he waited for his heart to stop thudding in his ears. His nipples rose up under his cotton shirt at the air-conditioned chill. He looked around. He was one foot from where he'd been all morning, but he thought he might as well be on a different planet.

The room seemed even bigger inside, maybe sixty-by-forty feet. The hardwood floor shone as if from within. The ceiling, molding, and window trim gleamed a snowy white. Seven aluminum beams ran from front to back just below the ceiling. The four walls were a deep marine blue and without adornment. An especially fat shaft of sunlight, particles swimming in it, fell upon the vast drafting table in the middle of the room. Danny approached it, then stopped. He looked right, then left, seeing who might be able to spy him from outside. The windows to the right, the ones facing the ocean, were unobstructed in that direction, the next house being set back quite a distance from the street. The windows to the left showed perhaps ten feet of space between this house and the neighboring one. But the women had pulled down the white blinds on these six windows. He turned around. The street tree just outside shielded his view from two windows, but the windows at each end of the front side were open to the street and the houses across the street, and the blinds were halfway up. He slipped to the ground. He crawled over to one window, then the other, slowly lowering the blinds while his body remained hidden beneath the windows, as if the Holy Ghost were doing this.

He stood up and breathed deeply, trying to smooth his jagged pulse. The room reeked of the odorless aroma of newness. Danny decided this was his favorite smell. He let the utter silence of the house fall upon him, just to be sure. Then, his feet barely grazing the floor, he walked over to the drafting table.

He looked at the computer first. The monitor was flat and larger than the television in Danny's living room at home. It was black, as were the curved keyboard, the huge printer/copying machine, and the two computer towers. A multicolored bouncing ball zipped noiselessly across the monitor's screen. There was a silver writing instrument on some papers beside the keyboard. Danny picked it up and its heaviness shocked his sweaty fingers. It was a metal drafting pencil. Danny slipped it into the pocket of his painter's pants without thinking. A truck went by outside and banged loudly as it boomed over a pothole. Danny jumped wildly. His vision narrowed and he turned his head, almost twisting his neck, to the door at the far end of the room. When he stopped trembling he sped back to the window. He let himself out, then yanked down the window, then the screen. He didn't think there was a way to pull the screen all the way down, but he wasn't sure if he would have done this even if he could have. He wanted to think that he would have.

Mr. Palmer seemed in a good mood when he stopped by close to 4:00 that afternoon.

"Oh . . . is it time?" Danny asked, looking down when Mr. Palmer called, "Hot one today," up to him.

"Just about quitting time," Mr. Palmer said. He smiled. "You're making good progress."

"Getting there," Danny said, sticking his wire brush, scraper, and sandpaper into his pockets. He felt the rigid stiffness of the drafting pencil as he did.

"You oughta be done with the third floor by the middle of next week, huh?

"Ahh . . . yeah. Ahh, I'm sorry; what did you say?"

"I said you oughta be done by the middle of next week. With the third floor."

"Ahh . . . yeah."

Danny told himself that night, and the next morning, that he wouldn't do it again.

He realized by lunchtime that he had to.

He wolfed his sandwich on the ladder and hurried through his scraping so he'd have more time. He slipped into the design room right after 1:00, when it became unbearable to not be in there. Again he lost his breath when he went in. He closed his eyes and stood motionless, listening to the quiet, breathing in the smell until his breath slowed. The blinds were still drawn, so he felt he could walk around with slightly less apprehension. Thinking more clearly today, he took off his boots and sweaty white socks and left them on the floor at the bottom of the window. The hardwood floor was cool and smooth against his damp, bare feet. He walked to the drafting table and leaned over to study the plans lying there. His blistered red fingers caressed the soft grayish-white paper, almost touched the indigo lines and circles and slashes denoting rooms and ceilings and fire walls and stairwells. Some kind of industrial building. Danny looked at the bottom of the large sheet of paper and saw BRENNAN PLACE written by hand in fat, blocky letters. The smell of the paper, its crispness, filled him with desire. He wasn't sure if life was encouraging him, showing him what he could have, or mocking him, shoving his face into what would never be his. *Dan-ny! Dan-ny!*

The smell of the black leather chair in the sun wafted up to him. He noticed a red tie covered with swirls of powder-blue paisleys slung over it—had that been there yesterday? He hadn't noticed it. Mr. Palmer said The Architect traveled a lot, and when he came home from traveling he'd most likely join his wife on Nantucket. But that was surmise on Mr. Palmer's part—in which case The Architect could come home at any second. There were always the urgent plans left at home, the early workday, the afternoon meeting that was canceled, the unendurable headache. A tingle of something swept through Danny. He couldn't be sure if it was excitement or fear. He wanted it to be fear.

He fingered the tie, running its rich, pillowy silkiness between his thumb and forefinger. Gooseflesh ran up his hand to his forearm. Yes, this was just the type of tie he would someday put on in his dressing area—quietly luxurious, understated but bold. A red light against the stainless white field of his starched shirt, shining bright as Daniel Sullivan went forth into the world—a man, an architect. A vague scent of cologne drifted up from the tie. It made Danny think of chattering, laughing people on a boat in tropical waters, the air throbbing to the hypnotic thud of consumerism as everyone exchanged business cards.

Without thinking of what he was doing, Danny doffed his baseball cap, then slid off his white long-sleeved jersey and the gray T-shirt beneath. He hadn't worn a tie since Grandmother Shea's funeral two and a half years ago, so it took him three tries to get it right. His fingers were trembling as they slung the knot up to his bare neck. The tie dangled just below his waist, its silkiness swishing against his bare chest and the fine golden hairs that ran down his stomach. He became painfully erect inside his tight painter's pants. He willed himself to ignore this. He felt his cheeks flush up.

A slam of a car door outside flooded him with panic. His heart leaped into overdrive. He found he couldn't move for a moment. He twisted his head in the direction of the street and felt something like electricity jolt through him when he saw the tracks his sweaty bare

feet had trailed across the flawless floor. He grabbed his jersey and
dropped to his knees, polishing the floor as he crawled backward to
the window. He slid the jersey on, picked up his socks and stuffed
them into his pocket, then stepped into his boots. He hit his head on
the window as he climbed outside to the ladder. He pulled down the
window and screen, then grabbed onto the ladder with wet hands, his
heart pounding. He didn't dare look down yet in case someone was
there, looking up. He reached for his scraper too quickly, knocking it
off the top ladder rung. He heard it clattering on the cement sidewalk
two seconds later.

"What, are you tryin' to kill me?" he heard. The sound froze him,
but there was something about the voice that kept his panic from becoming hysteria.

Holding tightly onto the sides of the ladder, Danny eased his eyes
downward. Billy McGillicuddy was standing three floors beneath
him, his arms on his narrow hips, squinting up at Danny.

"That musta been a lousy sub I made you; you ain't been back since
and now you're throwing shit at me!" he called up. He laughed easily.

"Ahh, s-sorry," Danny said. He realized he was smiling.

Billy bent over to pick up the scraper. *Go down!* Danny heard inside
him. It seemed what came naturally to others—the common rules of
friendly interaction—Danny always had to guess at.

His heart was still racing when he jumped off the bottom rung.

Billy was still smiling. He handed Danny the scraper. "Lucky for
me it wasn't a bucket of paint!" He laughed.

"Sorry," Danny repeated. "No, ahh, the s-sub was good, I just . . . I
been startin' earlier." He heard the lameness of this excuse as it came
out of his mouth. *I felt like an idiot because I didn't know about the Red Sox
trade.*

Billy waved him away like anything Danny said was okay. Billy's
light-brown hair was buzzed on the back and sides and longer on top,
cut in uneven bangs that fell casually onto his forehead. The sea
breeze played with them as Danny watched. Danny thought Billy's
eyes were the color of the sky he'd someday see from his dressing area.

"Hot as a mother today, huh?"

"Yeah," Danny answered.

"I was just heading out to Castle Island for my little lunch break; thought I'd come by and say hi." Billy rested his behind against the front wrought-iron fence.

Castle Island hadn't been an island in over a hundred years, since the quarter-mile causeway had been built connecting it to the mainland. Now it was a promenade surrounding an ancient grassy-lawned stone fort on the edge of the harbor where people walked, jogged, Rollerbladed, fished, and laid in the sun gobbling hot dogs and soft-serve ice cream from Sullivan's.

Danny was overwhelmed by Billy's friendliness. He looked up at him to meet his eyes and saw Billy staring at his neck. Billy immediately looked away.

The tie! You idiot—he sees the tie, sticking out of your collar!

"Yeah, it's a hot one, all right," Billy said.

Danny's mouth worked. Nothing came out but a gurgle. His heart started pumping wildly. Like clockwork, he knew his face was crimsoning. Billy met his eyes again at the strange noise Danny had made.

"Ahh . . . you okay there, Bert?" Billy asked in a purposely goofy Kermit the Frog imitation.

Billy seemed able, with just a smile, to cut through the heaviest disasters. It was impossible not to melt in the light of his ways.

"No, but I hope to be soon," Danny laughed. Billy laughed too and then punched Danny lightly on the shoulder.

"Come up and see me at the store, okay?"

Billy's lean was casual, but the back of his soft eyes seemed to be smeared with urgency.

"Ahh . . . yeah! Yeah, I'll come up tomorrow. For lunch," Danny said, surprised at the broadness of his own smile. "I usually take lunch at eleven-thirty."

"Good deal," Billy said, nodding his head. He kept his eyes on Danny's. Danny didn't look away. He didn't know if he could, even if he wanted to. Then Billy smiled, as if some kind of question had been answered. He again punched Danny lightly. "See ya then."

Billy strolled to his huge old Chevy parked ten feet away. The big dented door creaked loudly as he opened it and slipped in. He put on a pair of sunglasses that had been resting on the dashboard, then drove off with two fingers out the window making the peace sign.

Danny didn't go back in that day; the need didn't seem as great. The light-blueness of Billy seemed a flower he would pull out and sniff throughout the afternoon.

When Mr. Palmer came by at 4:00, he stumbled on a piece of scrapwood out front.

Me and Billy would never stumble, Danny thought.

"I can't believe they didn't clean up their mess yet," he said, turning back and looking down at what had tripped him. "You got a truck?"

"Ahh . . . no," Danny said. "My brother does though. Ahh . . . how come?"

"Well, there'll be an extra fifty bucks in your check this week if you clear this shit outta here by Friday," Mr. Palmer said. "It messes up the whole place."

Business must be really good, Danny thought.

"Okay," he said. "I'll try to do it tonight."

"Any sign of the guy today? The architect?"

Danny stiffened. He touched the rolled-up tie in his pocket just to make sure it wasn't hanging out.

"Ahh . . . no." He paused. "Why? Is he . . . what's he due back or something?"

"Oh, I have no idea," Mr. Palmer said. He turned and looked at Danny.

THAT NIGHT DANNY DREAMED he was wandering through The Architect's house. It was very early morning in his dream. The sun was just beginning to pour through the windows as it lifted itself over the cerulean ocean, the same color as Billy's eyes. Danny found himself in the kitchen of The Architect's house, opening the double-door aluminum refrigerator. Where the eggs should have been, in little cups scooped out on the door, instead were shining Christmas lights, the old-fashioned, big-bulbed kind. As Danny watched they lit up, brilliantly. Danny gasped, then woke. He sat up. The desire in him to go back into the house flared up, almost blinding him. He thought of Billy, and getting his lunch at McGillicuddy's, and a struggle began. He could almost hear a bell ring. He writhed over onto his stomach as if he were wrestling. Then he felt it, silky against his stomach and thigh.

All he was wearing under his race car sheets and plaid quilt was the red tie, wrapped around his hard waist like a belt. He would've worn it around his neck but George might have seen it in the morning when he got up. Danny sat up and squinted at his alarm clock. It was twenty-five minutes before seven. Too early to get up but too late to go back to sleep. George was already gone. He reached down and rubbed the dangling part of the tie against his stiff penis. He groaned lowly at the sensation. When he came he moaned, "Fuck you, fuck you, fuck you."

HE MOVED THE LADDER over to the last window on the third floor front around 11:00. He'd been struggling all morning with his desire. But he was winning. When he got to the top of the ladder he saw through the window his gray T-shirt on the floor beside The Architect's drafting table, as if it had been taken prisoner. In his panic at hearing Billy's car door slam yesterday he'd left it there.

Well, that ended that. He had to go back in, *now*. If The Architect came home abruptly, if the woman returned for . . . for anything, a doctor's appointment, a needed phone number—

Once inside, he took his boots off, but not his socks. He had to wait, again, for the breathless thrill to pass. He walked over to the drafting table. He picked up his shirt. He brought it to his face. It still smelled like him, but there was an additional aroma to it, a whiff of this place that had seeped in overnight. Danny thought this was how he might smell in the future.

There was a yellow Post-it note on the table he hadn't seen yesterday. DON'T FORGET MELANSON PLANS, written in printed, blue-inked letters.

"Yeah, don't fuckin' forget," Danny mumbled.

He sat down in the leather chair. It was warm from the sun and seemed to wrap itself around him, welcoming him. He placed his arms on the armrests. He rolled back a bit on its wheels, then forward toward the computer, at the same time that a US Airways MetroJet, carrying The Architect, was landing half a mile away at Logan International Airport.

Danny began idly flicking through the neon pages of the black metal Rolodex next to the computer. It seemed every listing ended in the words "group" or "associates." Or listed a company whose name reminded Danny of Greek battles he'd studied in junior-high history. *Jane Dunhill, Vision Group Architects; R. Klemp Associates; Timothy Winston, Zylaces Corporation.* No one was listed individually—people didn't seem to be people alone, but physical embodiments of mysterious, majestic forces behind them, like nervous priests speaking for an uncertain but all-powerful God.

He closed the Rolodex and sat back in the chair. Danny fantasized about bringing in one of his own designs—he'd shown no one, ever—and leaving it here on The Architect's desk. The Architect would be astounded. Impressed. *Whose work is this? This is. . . . It's fantastic!* He'd be astonished when he learned this was a kid's work, a kid who'd never had one minute of drafting lessons or architecture school.

So, where are you going in September?

No—he wouldn't say that. These people turned nouns into verbs. *I'll be summering on Nantucket . . .*

Where will you be collegeing in September?

Nowhere.

Don't be ridiculous; you have to.

I didn't get in anywhere.

They didn't know how talented you are. How could they know? I know people. Let me make some calls.

Well, there's this other problem, see: money.

Let me take care of that for you. Come here. Kiss me—

Danny shook his head. The Architect's smiling face faded, but not before it became Billy's.

Danny held his fingers over the computer, pretending to type. He wondered if The Architect ever worked up here late at night. Of course he did. He tried to see him, the moon spilling into the room like music. Danny wondered what The Architect wore on those occasions. A robe, white as the moonlight. Or boxers, silky expensive ones that gave you shivers just to slide them on. Or maybe just white briefs, like Danny—tight against the smooth, warm thighs—

Danny's eyes shifted.

He turned his head and looked toward the end of the room, to the open door. Through the door were stairs. Going down. To the bedroom.

As he slipped down the noiseless carpeted stairway, Danny tried to remember if his heart had ever pounded this crazily. The stairs turned a stained-glass-windowed corner, then came to a maroon-walled rest at a hall. Beside him was a door, half-open. The hall was sunny but the room through the gaping doorway was dark. He pushed open the door with his fingers. It was the bedroom.

"I'll be right back," he told the empty room.

He found the next flight, descended the stairs into an orange-walled front parlor, and made his way into the kitchen, which took up the entire back of the house. The floor was tiled with black-and-white stone. A vast oven, bigger than those in the neighborhood pizza parlor Danny went to, sat in the middle of the room like a landlocked ship. Dozens of dull pots and pans hung from wooden rafters, and the entire back wall was a honeycomb-like wine rack. Danny counted one row of bottles across, then a row down, and multiplied. There were over 2,000 bottles of wine in the kitchen.

The refrigerator wasn't where it had been in his dream. It *was* stainless steel and double-doored. He looked around. A maroon sweater was draped over one of the four chairs surrounding the butcher-block table. Another yellow Post-it note glowed on the table, beside some magazines Danny had never heard of. He leaned closer to the note. The writing was different from the note in the design room.

> Peter—
> You're such an asshole for what you said on the phone.

The note was unsigned. "Asshole" was underlined with two quick thick strokes. Danny was impervious to any unrelated stimuli at this point; it could've been a shopping list for the effect it had on him.

With a burst he began opening cabinets and pulling out drawers, taking a mindless inventory of everything he saw. There seemed to be an endless amount of things to put on food—rosemary balsamic vinegar of Modena, Thai peanut butter paste, extra virgin first cold-pressed olive oil—but no food itself. He marveled at the unique weirdness of people—their decision to put rolls of unopened paper towels in a drawer marked BREAD.

He finally walked over to the refrigerator and swung open the double doors while The Architect stepped into a cab, brushing the crumbs from his in-flight meal off his salmon-colored tie.

There were no Christmas lights inside the refrigerator, nor any egg-holding trays. Maybe they didn't make them like that anymore. A sigh blew out from him, and Danny realized it was one of relief. The left side of the refrigerator was the freezer. Three skinny Lean Cuisine boxes were stuck-stacked frozen one on top of the other, and a mountain of small geometrically-correct ice cubes spilled from a fertile black hole at the rear. The refrigerator's other side contained three jugs of spring water, a wilting head of celery, and a tippy, nearly empty pint of light cream. He grabbed one of the jugs of water, took off the blue plastic cap, and guzzled from the mouth of it. Then he shut the doors and slipped back upstairs, his step and eyes full of purpose.

His heart was pounding hard again as he stepped inside the bedroom. It was about half the size of the design room. The bed was huge and seemed to float above the hardwood floors and Oriental rug. Like the drafting table upstairs, the bed sat in the middle of the room. Four-posted, with a mustard-colored canvas canopy on top, it looked a hundred years old. Unlike Danny's at home, this bed was made, and tasseled pillows, seven of them of different sizes and colors, rested at the head. The room smelled of the slightly rotting flowers that sat in a round zinc vase on a nightstand beside the bed. Danny fingered one of the bedposts while he stared at the bed, wondering what dramas were played out here. Beyond the bed an antique table with a Tiffany lamp on top of it looked out a window. Beyond that a double archway led into another area. Danny could see a raised tub with large powder blue tiles around it. He stepped through the archway and took a step up. Here was a Jacuzzi, in a gleaming-fixtured bathroom bigger than Danny's bedroom. A tube of whitening toothpaste with its cap off gleamed on the pedestal sink. Off one side of the bathroom was an open area, thickly carpeted, with mirrored closets on two opposite walls. Danny felt a tightness in his stomach. The dressing area.

He took off his clothes in the bathroom, watching himself in the mirror as his long-sleeved jersey, then his white T-shirt, slid over his head. He unbuttoned his white painter's pants. He didn't even have to unzip them; they fell over his thirty-inch waist to the bathroom floor with a slight rumpling sound. He stepped out of them one leg at a time, then kicked them away. He leaned one hand on the silky corn-flower blue wallpaper and pried off one sweaty sock, then the other. As he tossed them away he saw that they were mismatched.

It was midday and the traffic coming back from the airport was minimal.

Danny walked into the dressing area with a pounding heart. He wiped his wet hands against the back of his white briefs. He stood in the center of the room. Without turning his head, he could see the back of himself in the mirrors on the closet doors behind him. He slipped his thumbs into the waistband of his briefs. Keeping an eye on his backside, as if he were watching someone else, he lowered the briefs down slowly. Then he bent down as he stepped out of them. He brought them to his forehead and wiped away his sweat. Then he dropped them to the floor. A pennant on the wall before him, above the closets, said HARVARD SQUASH CLUB. Danny thought this was like racquetball, except you wore all white. He slung his right arm through the odorless air, paddling an imaginary ball with an imaginary racquet. Yet he felt phony as he did it, as if he were acting for an audience.

Danny turned around slowly, examining the person in the mirror. He studied each curve and limb of the white body, how everything moved together in such seamless architectural harmony. Then he faced the mirror again. He started at the feet, then raised his eyes upward, slowly. When his eyes met the eyes in the mirror he couldn't look away. His breath was coming in chops and his hands began trembling.

He opened the closet door in front of him, then shut it immediately at the sight of the blouses and career suits, the army of flats and heels in tight rows on the closet floor awaiting marching orders. He turned around and pulled open the other closet's doors. A smell of cedar gushed out as if to greet him. He heard himself gasp. His blistered, sunburned hand moved slowly, reverently closer, then ran itself down the richness of suits, dress shirts, ties, pants, and summer jerseys, enough of the latter to outfit an entire golf course by the sea.

He pulled out the darkest suit from the dozen or so hanging there, and laid it reverently upon a ladder-back chair with an oval seat that was resting in the corner.

Two lines of built-in wooden drawers rose from floor to ceiling at the closet's end. Danny swallowed hard. He looked around, found the light switches he was looking for at the room's far end, then flicked them up. A runway row of recessed lights burst to life from the ceiling. Their brightness made him jump. He was young enough that his body looked even better under the harsh lighting. He marveled at how the white flesh was shining in its reflected smoothness in one place, then became thick with black hair only inches away. He wondered how the hair on The Architect's body arranged itself. In his mind's eye Danny saw a plan for a male body drawn up on paper similar to the thick sheets on the drafting table upstairs, denoting exactly where each hair should be placed, how long it must be, and whether straight, or tight with spiraled curls.

He turned back to the drawers and eased the middle one open, pulling on the pewter rosebud fixture. It slid exactly open on noiseless rollers. A dozen or more pair of black socks were arranged as precisely as cloned fruit in a box. Danny lifted a pair, rubbing the material between his fingers. Then he put them on.

He opened three more drawers—of silk handkerchiefs, white athletic socks, and a shining array of cufflinks—before he found the underwear drawers. The white T-shirts were a brand Danny had never heard of, but they looked like any other white T-shirts, crewnecked and size Men's Large. They seemed to be a little softer than what Danny was used to. There were two drawers for underpants, one filled with silk and cotton boxers, the other with white briefs, size 34, not folded, but spread out face up. He ran his fingers along the elastic waistband of one before taking it out of the drawer. He opened them up to put them on, then realized he couldn't get dressed without taking a shower first. He never put on clean clothes—even his painting rags—before taking a shower. A thousand inner groans at what he was doing all fell away to the power that was driving him on. He pulled off the dark socks and laid them, with the white briefs, tenderly upon the dark suit on the chair. He walked back into the bathroom, his erection divining the way.

He turned the water on and ran his hand under the spray, which is why he didn't hear the car pull up out front, or its door slamming. There was no "H" or "C" on the black steel tap that jutted arrogantly out of the blue-tiled shower stall. He couldn't get the temperature right. When he heard the rapping on one of the front windows, and a voice, blurred by the water, he jumped so much that he banged his head on the shower door. Something that felt to him like liquid ice shot through his head.

Someone!

For the rest of his life he always marveled at how quickly he moved then. He couldn't get the water to turn off for what seemed a minute, but later he realized it was probably only seconds, albeit the longest of his life. He pulled on his painter's pants first, shoving his briefs and T-shirt and socks into his ample back pockets. He pulled on his jersey and saw the gooseflesh on his stomach. He stampeded into the dressing area. He put The Architect's briefs back into the T-shirt drawer with the T-shirt, but had no time to correct his mistake. The Architect's socks he left on. He pounded up the third-floor stairs, his breath ahead of him. He stopped at the entrance to the design room, paralyzed by the sight of a pair of hands descending the ladder outside. The afternoon sun pouring through the windows blinded him. He grabbed yesterday's T-shirt from beside The Architect's black leather chair, then ran across the room and stepped into his boots. He slid open the window and crawled out, grabbing onto the wobbling ladder. He pulled the window down, then the screen. The screen came all the way down, and it did click into place when it reached the bottom. Danny grabbed onto both edges of the ladder.

His breath was coming so fast, he thought he would pass out. He didn't move, but waited for what would happen next. He knew he wouldn't move again until something happened.

"*There* you are!" came hurtling up at him.

Billy. At the bottom of the ladder.

Danny still couldn't move; there was too much flying through his head, like flecks of paint chips.

"It's just me," Billy called up. "How are ya today?"

Danny gulped. He took a deep breath.

"P-pretty good," he called. If his heart would stop racing—

"What, d'you stand me up for lunch?"

"Ahh . . . ahh, no. No."

"Well, I'm ready when you are, cowboy."

When Danny was finally about halfway down the ladder, Billy said, "I was looking for you; you didn't come up to the store so I came down. I made us some subs."

Danny stopped and looked down. Billy was wearing a kelly green T-shirt that said ST. BRENDAN'S on the front and the number seven on the back. The sleeves had been hacked off and a shamrock the size of a half-dollar was tattooed on Billy's left arm, right where it became his shoulder.

Danny smiled. A bead of sweat dripped from his nose. Billy smiled back.

"I figgered we could go out to The Island for lunch?" Billy said, the sentence ending in a questioning rise.

"S-sure," Danny said, stepping off the ladder. He could still hear his heart in his ears, thudding away. He took a deep breath and exhaled loudly.

"Where were you, out back?"

"Ahh . . . y-yeah," Danny said. He didn't trust himself to say any more.

"Yeah, I figured you must be. I climbed up the ladder and knocked on one of the windows to try and make some noise. I figgered you musta been out back or washing your hands on the side there or somethin'."

"Yeah," Danny repeated. He opened his mouth, then shut it. Billy smiled.

"Like I say, I was waitin' for you up the store . . . then I figgered you musta wanted to take a late lunch." He paused. There was a depth to his eyes that Danny hadn't noticed before.

"The time . . . kind of ran away from me," Danny said. "It . . ." He held up his hands.

"C'mon," Billy said encouragingly, tossing his head toward his car but keeping his eyes on Danny's. "Let's get outta here."

Danny nodded. He looked around, up at the ladder, at the house. He gulped again, took another deep breath, then walked over to the old Chevy.

He got into Billy's car. An old newspaper was on the floor. A red pine tree air freshener with the cellophane halfway down swung from the radio's tuning knob. A white paper bag sat on the middle of the seat.

"Lunch!" Billy laughed, patting the bag as he hopped in and started up the car. Danny heard a door slam behind him. He turned as Billy looked in his rearview mirror. A man carrying a black travel bag was moving up the walk, away from a yellow cab. Danny couldn't see the averted face of The Architect. He let out a gasp. Billy turned to him quickly and Danny studied him, wondering how smart Billy was, remembering how The Architect's house could be seen from McGillicuddy's Spa.

"What?" Billy asked, tilting his head quizzically. His smile was a little different this time.

Danny could only jerk his thumb behind him and shake his head. Billy's eyes lingered on Danny's.

They pulled away. As they turned onto the breezy boulevard, Danny felt his breath easing into a normal pattern. Billy's baggy shorts came down to his knees and Danny stole looks at Billy's right leg as it worked the gas, the brake. He looked up once and Billy was staring at him, smiling again.

"That's my leg," he laughed, slapping his knee.

Danny's breath caught.

"S'okay," Billy said softly. God, he was beaming. He turned his head back to the road.

"Really, it's okay," he repeated.

THEY PULLED INTO the parking lot at Castle Island and got out. Billy laughed, for no apparent reason. He grabbed a Frisbee from the backseat.

"I like to throw junk around," he told Danny over the car roof.

Billy knew many people they came across: the housewives out for their power walks or the young mothers or fathers pushing strollers. Everyone asked about his father. Gulls raked the air overhead, squawking when someone chucked them food. The sky and sea were the same color, and radiant, as if the one had just rinsed the other. There was a hint of approaching fall in the air and light.

They picked a spot on the luxurious, sun-warmed grass on the hill behind the stone castle, and sat down. Billy laughed again for no apparent reason. The harbor opened up before them like an expanding dream. The harbor islands were a light-blue smudge on the horizon.

Danny became aware of a lightness inside him.

Big cottony clouds drifted across the sky, as slowly as the ships below them easing out of the harbor.

"I remembered that you liked the Boyd's potato chips," Billy said, handing the small bag to Danny. He pulled out one sandwich, then another. A "D" written with a fat red pencil marked Danny's.

"Thanks."

"I figgered we could just split our drink," Billy said, wiggling himself into a cross-legged sitting position and sliding a big green plastic bottle from the bag. A sea breeze gushed at the bag and Billy lunged at it, laughing again, before it could blow away. "I sure hope you like Mountain Dew," he said.

"I love it," Danny said, smiling. A radiance sprang up around the patch of grass surrounding them. They began eating in an easy silence.

"How . . . how do you like the store? How are things at the store?" Danny asked halfway through lunch.

"I really like it," Billy said. He turned his head away and burped lowly. He smiled. "Oops. Excuse me. That'd be polite in the Middle East. In three more years, I'll own it. The store I mean, not the Middle East. How's about you? You still want to be an architect?"

Danny's head lurched. Billy laughed.

"Naw, I ain't a mind reader. I just remember your brother, George, told me one time that's what you wanted to do. He said you were crazy about it."

"Oh, yeah."

"That's great. I do this Habitat for Humanity thing once a month. You know about that?"

"Ahh . . . I think so."

"A bunch of people get together and build, like, affordable houses for people. They're always looking for architects to help out." Billy paused and scratched the blond stubble on his chin. "Maybe you'd like to come with me next time."

Danny could feel something shift behind his stomach. There were other people in the world. There were more important rooms than dressing areas.

"I'd like that!" he blurted. Then he blushed for appearing so zeal-ous.

"Good deal, then," Billy said easily. He put a whole chip in his mouth, then crunched down on it. At the same time he reached his hand across the distance between them, and softly brushed Danny's chin with his closed fist. It seemed to Danny that the harbor behind Billy contracted, and contained now only the two of them. A thing fluttered inside, like birds' wings.

BILLY TURNED HIS HEAD again and smiled out at the harbor, the ocean. A soft breeze mowed through the grass, then flickered through Billy's sun-bleached leg hair. "I come out here a lot. It's about my fa-vorite place in the world," he said.

"You seen much of the world?" Danny asked.

Billy shrugged and turned back to Danny.

"I did a quick tour in the Marines, three and a half years. I seen a few places." His smile faded. Danny noticed how long Billy's eyelashes were. "I didn't really care for it. I like it back here. I like it at the store. I like giving people what they need. I like it out here. You can just sit back and . . . look at the sky with quiet eyes."

Yet Billy's eyes weren't looking at the sky right now. They were softly focused on Danny's.

Danny felt a smile pulling at the edges of his mouth.

"C'MON," BILLY SAID after lunch, grabbing the Frisbee and standing up. "Time to work off them chips."

In a minute they were running. Danny stopped to kick off his boots after Billy shed his sneakers. Danny saw that he was still wearing The Architect's black socks. He pried them off and started laughing.

"What?" Billy called, twenty feet away. He stopped and put his hands on his hips, holding the Frisbee.

"What what?" Danny asked back.

"What's so funny?"

"I . . . I was just thinking," Danny said. "Some people . . . . Some people have houses full of pots and pans, and no food." He stopped. "Can I tell you stuff?"

Danny was surprised at his own boldness.

Billy laughed, then became serious. He took a few steps toward Danny.

"You sure can," he said. "I think. . . . You know what, Danny Boy? I think you'll be surprised at the stuff we end up telling each other."

For the catching of a breath, Danny couldn't answer.

"Ahh . . . what was I saying? I forget now."

"People with pots and pans, and no food."

"Oh, yeah. There's some people with tons of pots and pans, and no food. And . . . and Rolodexes full of phone numbers, but no friends to call." He stared at Billy. "You know Rolodexes? Those things with numbers?"

Billy held Danny's eyes for what seemed a very long time. "I do. And who needs that?" he finally answered. He smiled again. "Okay, Danny Boy—go out for a long one!"

Danny turned and raced up the grassy hill. Turning his head as he ran, he saw the Frisbee uncoiling through the blue air above him. Danny cried out and redoubled his speed. As he caught it in a dive to Billy's *whooo!* he was thinking he'd build a fort, a little house, from the old scrapwood he had dumped in his small back yard at Mr. Palmer's urging. Maybe he'd drag his mother's basement couch out there after he built it.

It was kind of dumb, but he'd do it anyway. He'd start designing it tonight. He'd bring Billy there when it was done.

Billy would like it; he knew he would.

It probably wouldn't have a dressing area.

Lughead

If time is relative, why can't we see the future?

Stephen Hawking

I played up there. That is a total hack league; better wear shin guards.

Up at that place there, Hockeytown, the Hockeytown rink. No, it's on Route One there. Whatever you call it, the Lynnway or something. I dunno maybe not the Lynnway.

Naw, nothing special. I was coming back from a back injury, that was when I was roofin'. MacDonald Roofin', you know them? What's his name worked there, Richie's cousin. Yeah, Richie Corbett. That's a fuckin' hard job. You ever try liftin' one of them shingle packs? There's like sixty pound of weight there, maybe more, and you're going up that ladder all day like a monkey. Fuckin' sucks. Specially at the end of the day, or in summer. Brutal in summer. Throw in customers with attitude and it can turn out to be a real shit sandwich of a job.

No I didn't fall or nothing, I missed a step on the ladder there and the shingles started sliding and I was like holding onto them? And like it just didn't occur to me at first to let 'em go, let 'em drop but then like we're both sliding off the ladder cuz I lost my balance so I figured hey I better let these shingles go man or I'm gonna be going with 'em.

It was this rich lady's house in Belmont. She was a college professor at Harvard. I never met a real one of them before except like in the movies. She came out and roared at us cuz the shingles I dropped crushed one of her bushes, one of her favorite bushes. *That bush has been in our family for thirrrrrrrrrty years,* she said. Like I did it on purpose. Not that smart if you ask me, like I fuckin' did it on purpose. The nosy neighbor next door who watched us all day told us the lady taught ethics. I thought about that the rest of the day, the subway ride home too and I finally found the thought that was trying to get me: there's a thing, and then there's like the study of a thing.

You know what I mean?

I just wrenched it or something, but better than fallin', right? So the next day I can't even move. It wasn't a union job or nothing so no work, no pay. So I was out for a bit, and of course I couldn't play hockey that winter, so then Mikie calls me up one day late winter and says there's this floor hockey league startin' up up at Hockeytown there and was I interested. Like it might be a good idea to get into this league so the next year I could play hockey again and not be too out of shape? It was like this spring league. So I said no, but then he called again like two weeks later and said they just needed one more guy so what the fuck. What are you gonna do. Yeah, I was back to work then, my back was fine, I just didn't really think I'd like that league. Yeah a good job, union and everything, my cousin got me on the Big Dig. Still there too. Hard work? Yeah, course it is, wicked hard, what d'you think. In them fuckin' tunnels all day, bustin' your ass? We lose like two guys a year, on average. Pipe-fittin'. Oh I get it, when all that money shit happened, that Big Dig money scandal there, that's what you mean, like we sat around all day and that's why there was those fuckin' overruns or whatever you call 'em. Huh. I can tell you never worked a day in your life cuz you'd know, when them scandals happen, it's never the guys doin' the work get the money. I gotta tell you everything? Guinea boss too. You never wanna get a guinea boss. My father used to say that too and damn he was right, don't ask me why.

You're half-Italian? Well whatdya want, I speak the truth. Ask anybody. There's guineas and there's Italians, the Italian lady next door told me that. Just like there's Irish and there's Thick Micks. Everybody, you know, all nationalities. I ain't gonna name you no more in case you're half that too, since you're so fuckin' sensitive. And I could, too.

So no, that league there, I just didn't wanna play floor hockey. I mean, floor hockey? You play hockey all your life and then you're playing floor hockey, you know what I mean? Like a broad's game or somethin', but then the first night I was like couldn't believe it, I was fuckin' suckin' air like crazy, runnin' up and down and all. Wicked hack league, and some pretty good fights too, and usually the ref is like a guy from one of the teams so he gets into it too, he's not gonna stop it. Wicked hack league. I couldn't wait to play the next week, you know? And then you know afterward, you go out, have a few brews and the guys you were fightin' with your singing with after, you know. Guy shit. So that lasted like . . . ten weeks?. . . . Wait a minute, we had . . . there was like four weeks we played, then like a holiday or something . . . no, nothing big but like one of them presidents holidays or something where everybody's supposed to go shoppin' . . . and then we played . . . lemme see, we played Lenny's Auto Glass on like the third week before the season ended and they were like the best and we almost beat them, cuz I remember we were tied with them going into the game for the best record and we had like two more weeks after that and we were like seven-and-oh then or something. . . . What difference does it make? It makes a lotta fuckin' difference! Who's tellin' the story here? You ain't old enough to have any good stories. Oh, you think so? All right well, when I'm fuckin' done you can have the floor, okay? But in the meantime just shut the fuck up and try to remember when I'm talkin' the only interruption allowed is applause, okay? Fuckin' smack you.

Were we all from Southie, on the team? No no, not all. Lemme see, there was Fitzy, and the two Sullys, and one of their cousins Tommy I think but he never showed up after the third week, I forget what the fuckin' problem was . . . I dunno, something with his girlfriend or something, they were getting married and they had to go to these marriage lessons at her church or something. . . . Everybody was like, marriage lessons? What do they, show you porn or something? You seen enough of that already, man.

He musta been whipped . . . then ahh . . . who else . . . oh, there was Phil of course, he used to drive me every week to the games, I'd ride with him . . . yeah . . . yeah, so what if I did? Who fuckin' told you I lost my license? Whatdya mean, you heard? Heard from who? Yeah, well . . . like they say, whatever. Fuckin' whatever, I was stupid, awright? So like—you did? When? Did you get it back yet? I was gonna say, I hope you fuckin' got it back because I seen you drive here, I seen you pullin' up with your car there when you first got here. Yeah, I seen you. Hey, what can I say, it's no way to go. No, it'll ruin your life. That's why I don't drink anymore at all. Three years, yup. You don't wanna go there. I'm tellin' you, you don't have to.

So no, there was like five of us from town and—awright six, what the fuck are you now, a mathematician? So like five or six of us, and the other guys were like from here and there, friends, cousins, whatever. So we were playin' that Lenny's Auto Glass team and they were like numero uno, they were the best. Won the thing every year, they'd been playing together for years, had their own jackets and uniforms and shit. I mean like the pants too, everything. We just had some T-shirts Ronnie's girlfriend made up that didn't come til halfway through the season anyways. And they were fuckin' purple if you can believe it, with some fuckin' beauty school thing on the inside. I don't know, some fuckin' thing. They were like rejects and when everyone bitched Ronnie's girlfriend she was in the stands she like yells out, *what the fuck do you want for free,* which was another fuckin' problem because we'd all given Ronnie like fifteen bucks each for uniforms at the beginning of the season but I guess he blew it up his nose but that's another fuckin' story.

But that night there when we were playin' them, that first place team, that Lenny's team there—jeez, you should'a seen them. You play sports at all? They were like, it was amazing to watch them, they had it all going on, I mean we were okay but mostly hackers and kinda physical, but they'd like pass the puck like boom boom boom next guy boom and like before you knew it they'd scored, it was like they had it down, you wouldn't even see the puck and boom it was in the net. Course Sully kinda sucked in the goal, we didn't really have a goalie so we just stuck Sully in there cuz he's so fuckin' fat and he like was spillin' outta that goal and you had to really aim it just right to get it by him and whenever a shot came near him he'd close his eyes and duck and go *Jesus Christ!* wicked loud, you could hear it all over the place.

But they had like this one guy on the team—you ever . . . I mean, you ever have that experience, ESP or whatever they call it déjà vu, where like you look at someone and it's like you've known them, even though you don't and you know you've never seen them before? Something about them? You know what I mean at all? Because I don't know, they had this guy on their team, he like played center, he was the like the brains of their team, he was the one who set everybody up, moved them around. Didn't say anything really, just like bark out a name once in a while and jerk his head in a certain direction like and all his teammates would move. Tallish, maybe six foot, six one, dark hair, medium length, somewhat . . . wavy. Dark Irish lookin'. Kinda stern-looking face, quiet type but . . . like I say the brains kinda. So, we're playin' them, right, and like I say this was like this really physical league, oh but before that, so like we're playin' them and right before the game started you know we're like checking out the competition and they're looking at us and we're looking at them and everybody's kinda like goofin' and tryin' to pysch the other team out and everything, and I just happened to be looking at this team and I was squirting some water in my mouth and I happened to be looking at this guy for a second, that dark Irish guy and then he turned and looked at me across the floor there, and I had this like *where do I know him from* thing going on, and I'm thinkin' maybe around town, but no cuz I asked Jackie I says does he look familiar to you at all cuz Jackie like knows everybody in town and he was like no, I never seen him before why, and I didn't answer but then I knew he wasn't from around town, and then I'm like is he on the Big Dig with me, but then no, I knew it wasn't that, and then I kinda gave up cuz the game started and like five seconds into the game boom they slap one right at Sully and like I say thank God he's so fuckin' fat because it would'a been like ten-to-nothing in the first ten minutes, all you could hear was that dark Irish guy on the other team barkin' out orders and Sully screamin' *Jesus Christ!* every ten seconds when they took a slap shot at him. Yeah, they are plastic but lemme tell you those fuckin' things sting, specially you catch one in the face.

But like I say it was a pretty physical league even though it wasn't supposed to be and as the game really got going we started hitting them a little and figgering out their moves, and so the game was like really gettin' intense, but still it seemed like whenever I had a second to catch my breath I'd look at this guy and he was like lookin' at me. But when me and him crossed paths, it was like no one gets near you in this league without hitting you a bit, taking like a hit at you, not a huge check but more like a good bump, and of course like I say your shins take a walloping with them sticks and all. You should'a seen my shins for like that whole spring, Denise used to say *Oh honey* all the time when she'd see my shins, but whenever me and this dark Irish guy came in close to each other we'd hit each other, but it was more like a lean, like a leaning into each other, and both of us trying to like lean harder and both of us like equally strong, but it's like when we did that this ESP thing again like, like . . . it was weird, it was like we were twins or something and now we were reunited—no no, we didn't look alike at all, are you listenin' at all? Me with this fuckin' red hair? I fuckin' told you, he was dark Irish. I don't mean like that I mean like when you read in the paper sometimes about twins being separated at birth and then they meet and there's like this, this like energy or something when they touch each other, like psychicness or something. You know what I mean? And I'm like, where the fuck do I know this guy from? Even his smell smelled familiar. Not to be gross.

Yeah, they did, they beat us, but it was like three-to-one or something like that, it was wicked close because they got their last goal with like five seconds left, and afterwards they were saying how it was like the best game they'd played in in like five years, and they couldn't believe it because we were like a new team and—yeah, I got the only goal for us, how'd you know?—and they expected we'd be like this pushover team, and after the game this guy from the other team, the dark Irish guy there, was like leaning his chin on top of his hands which were resting on top of his stick, and I said to myself, I know that gesture too, I know that, I know that. I know it sounds weird. And he was like talking and smiling and being real friendly after the game with our guys, this thin-lipped very friendly smile and a nod of agreement at everything that was said which was like so different from how he was during the game, he was like so intense during the game you wouldn't believe it. But then Phil my ride had to get going because of some reason I forget now, so we like took off, but I could hear Sully say you guys going to get a drink to the other team and they said yeah, we're going here, we always go here, they named this place and said why don't you come, but it was some place like in Lynn or something, they were all like from up by that way and then no one said nothing because no one really wanted to drive home all the way from Lynn after a few frosties, but all this time this dark Irish guy is like looking at me back and forth to see if I was gonna go I think, and I didn't know what to do and Phil was in a rush *C'mon, c'mon* so we just left, but I think as I turned away, just like as I turned away he nodded at me, just like this one half little jerk of his head but I couldn't be sure.

Locker rooms? Yeah they had locker rooms. They'd only open one of them so both teams shared it, and some of the guys would keep some of their stuff there maybe during a game, or change quick after a game but usually people didn't shower after a game, I dunno some of the guys did, the place was a little dumpy and had that hockey locker smell if you know what I mean. Like moldy laundry from Alaska, it always reminds me of. Not the cleanest place I ever been in. So no, we'd usually take off right after a game, or maybe just change our shirts and towel off real quick, though once in a while someone would take a quick shower, not usually though. So we took off that night like I say right away. Phil had something, I forget now.

I always wanted to play the saxophone. I know that sounds weird. I mean, I do play the saxophone and I played it then, but not too much because . . . well see, they put me in the technical school. I didn't really wanna go but everyone called me *Lughead, Lughead.* Dennis McDaid started it, he was always makin' up fuckin' names for people and it just stuck, and I'm not sayin' I'm Einstein or nothing but I didn't want to go to the techy school, I wanted to play the saxophone but.

Never-you-mind, Ma used to say when I was a kid and she'd see how bummed out I was, Lughead and Techy School and the teachers all dismissive-like. I know my boy, she used to say, and in time you can see through a brick wall. See right into your future. And someday you'll meet somebody who can see that in you.

I'd try to remember that over the years, like when I finally dropped out of high school and then the Marines and everything, tried to think she was right when it was *Lughead, Lughead, what the fuck are you doing.* Just cuz I liked to read comic books.

So like I was sayin', the saxophone. Sometimes when it was late but not too late, or if I was riled or something, I used to go out on the fire escape there just outside my bedroom in my old apartment on West Sixth Street and play my sax a little. Not too loud because Mr. McGreevey next door would like . . . what? No he wouldn't like call the cops or nothing, but he'd like slam down his window at exactly ten-thirty, like you could set fuckin' Big Ben by when he would slam down the window, so I'd never play it after ten-thirty. But I'd go out there in my bare feet and no shirt on—I don't know why, but I always had to have bare feet and no shirt on when I played out on the fire escape. Even sometimes when Denise was over, we'd be like—she was my girlfriend then—we'd be like, you know, all romantic or whatever and I'd just get up when we were done, pull on a pair of pants and lift up the window at the end of the bed and slide out to the fire escape and play my saxophone. Yeah, they were always pants when I played the saxophone, never shorts—I don't know why—long pants and bare feet and no shirt on, what can I tell you I'm just weird. You must have weird things like that too and you don't know why.

This'll sound weird too, but . . . oh, thanks, that's nice of you to say . . . yeah, I guess everybody does a little . . .what was I saying? Oh yeah, this'll sound a little weird, but it was like . . . no, we had a great sex life I guess. I mean, as compared to what, you know? What you see in the movies? But anyways, we'd be like close together, or watching a movie me and Denise , or lying in bed after we did it, and it was like, I had this weird thing. It was like, if I could just tell Denise that it bothered me, people calling me Lughead, then we'd always be together. If I could just tell her that, like . . . like confess it, you know, how much it kinda bothered me, it always bothered me growing up. I had this weird thing in my head that if I could tell her that, then we'd always be together, me and Denise. But see I was this certain me with her, you know? You know how like there's different me's that different people bring out in you? And I was this certain me with her, you know like a Saturday Night Me with her, picking her up in my black leather jacket and black shoes and nice gray turtleneck sweater and black dress pants a fresh haircut and big-ass pump from the gym and some nice cologne, and we'd be going out to dinner or down to one of them clubs in The Alley or down by Fanueil Hall there or whatever to be by ourselves or meet up with the others, and I was like holding the door and everything, and I was like twice as big as her, I was like this certain me with her . . . I know I'm not explaining it right . . . but it was like, I was like this—what'd you say, protector? Yeah—maybe a little, but that's not exactly what I mean, it wasn't all about that—I was like . . . like this certain me, and I could never seem to get out of that certain me when I was with her. But I knew that if I could say to her *Denise, lookit, it really bothers me when people call me . . .* see, I can't even say it now, pretendin' that I am! Isn't that fuckin' funny? I just can't do it! But if I told her how much it bothered me that they called me Lughead—I mean, it bothered me, but it didn't bother me that much, it wasn't so much about that—but if I could'a just said to her that thing, confessed to her that thing, then I would'a been able to be a different me with her, not just the Saturday Night Me, and I knew if I could do that then we would'a been together forever and we would'a gotten married. And on the other hand, I knew that if I couldn't say that to her, then we'd never get married, because I couldn't get married to someone who I couldn't be all of my me's with, or at least, more than one me, more than my Saturday Night Me. Follow? Which is why I guess I felt lonely a lot when I was with her. Funny, huh? Feeling lonely when you're with someone else, especially your main squeeze. So I never brought up the marriage thing, not even to like talk about it in the future as this like hypothetical thing we were looking at from a distance like, or whatever. No, she never did, she was so cool, she was way too cool to bring the subject up more than once. She'd just look at you, that kinda girl. Smart. But I know that's why—well, I'm gettin' ahead of myself here.

But I was gonna say, I'd go out on the balcony sometimes and play my saxophone. Oh anything, not like real songs really, just like, like how I was feeling like. Kinda slow and mellow stuff mostly, and I never knew what, because it seemed whatever I was feelin', it just came out when I'd put that tube up to my mouth. It'd all come out like. But it was one of these nights one time, hot wicked hot, and I think the McGreeveys was all away because it was like after ten-thirty, but it was so hot everyone like had their windows shut and the AC on or if they didn't, they had their windows open but they were still up because it was too hot to sleep, you know what I mean? Crickets going crazy—yeah, we got crickets in Southie—fans whirring, you could hear little-kid-screen-door-slamming three blocks over, one of them summer nights. Not a sea breeze at all, and usually we get the sea breeze in Southie. And like five houses down from me— this was over on West Sixth, I had this little apartment then over on West Sixth Street—no, my place was kinda a shithole but I didn't mind, I really liked it believe it or not it was wicked cheap. All alone, no one ever bothered me, kinda dark and small with a pointy ceiling from the roof. They couldn't rent it out because the trains went right by all day and half the night and the bed rattling, this one kitchen shelf rattling but not the others which was weird, and every time someone would visit they'd say *how come that shelf's empty* and I'd go like *watch this,* and I'd put this candy dish Ma gave me as a house gift with after-dinner mints in it but they were like dusty and stale now, and we wouldn't have to wait long, the train would come by and that dish would rattle like mental, rattle all the way to the end of the shelf and I'd have to catch it so it wouldn't smash off the end like.

So anyways. But you know I used to lie there and sometimes I'd be all bummed out, like *Lughead, Lughead!* I'd hear in my head, like jeering or whatever, but then I'd roll to the end of my bed and look out the window and wait for the subway to go zooming by, and it was like the faces would all fly by me, wicked fast but I'd see them all just for a second like they were freeze-frames or whatever you call it, and I'd tell myself, now all them people are going somewhere. They are doing something with their lives, even if they're just riding the subway. And so one night I figured instead of feeling sorry for myself I would get up and ride the subway, and when I did I seen this ad on the top there of the subway where they have like ads, and they had a little postcard you could take if you wanted to, and it was for this trade college and you could learn stuff, so that's how I started going to school to be a pipe fitter and got in the union and got a good job and all. You know what I mean?

But like I was saying—no, I don't go off on tangents! You make me go off on tangents with all your questions, you're like Sherlock Holmes with all your fuckin' questions—so I'm out on my fire escape this one hot summers night, and for some reason Denise wasn't over, she didn't come over every night, mostly just weekends and one night during the week she'd come over—and I'm playing my saxophone and being really mellow, and all of a sudden this light comes on in a window up on like someone's third floor like five houses down, and no I'm not no Peeping Tom or nothing but my eye just like *went there,* you know what I mean? and there's like no shades in this window, and I see this figure move across the window, like wicked blurry, and then this other figure or maybe the same figure, and like . . . I dunno, it was like this funny feelin' came over me, like I was a fly in the wall and no one could see me watchin' them, like this burnin' inside me or something. and then they come together, and there's this guy and a girl, it might'a been one of the Halloran boys, that used to be their house there but I didn't know anymore, and like, *Jesus Christ* I said to myself, they started like ripping, ripping each other's clothes off, like they were going *off!* And like my heart started thumping crazy and I got like this ping thing in my stomach, like a ball in my stomach was spinning and squirting out all this hot liquid, and this note on my saxophone came out like all screwy cuz I was just blowing a note then, and like at first the girl was like pushing the boy back a little, and they were both laughing, but then when he'd back off she would like start being really coy with him, she'd like take a piece of her hair, she had like medium brown hair, she'd take a piece of her hair and like shove it in his mouth, or like take her finger and stick it in her mouth and wet it and then run that wet finger down his body, and he had his shirt off white skin glaring from the electric bulb over them but she was still wearing like this black slip thing or something, like one of them Victoria's Secret things you know, and then he'd try and take it off her and she'd laugh and push him away again, but like then she'd start up again with him after she pushed him away.

The room was painted green, and I remember there was this calendar on the wall behind them, and once in a while they'd disappear outta my sight line and I'd be staring at this calendar going like *C'mon, c'mon where the fuck are yous?,* and I couldn't see the picture it had on it but it looked like a beach scene, and I remember thinkin' how weird it was that when I woke up that morning I had no idea I'd be spending the night staring at this calendar, like getting to know exactly what this calendar in a bedroom down the street looked like. Cuz I mean I couldn't look away, it was like . . . my eyes were like glued there, you know? I think anybody's would'a but maybe not, I felt a little guilty but it felt so good I wasn't even thinking about that til later. And I kept playing my saxophone, but now like I was playing to how they were acting, my music was like all slow and kinda funky and . . . and hot like, and then all of a sudden the guy comes back into my sight, and he leaves the room, he like opens this door and leaves the room and he's like totally naked, and then while he's gone I see the girl again, and she's naked too but while he was gone she sticks her face in real close to the calendar, and then I see it isn't a calendar at all but a mirror, it's like this mirror with a picture or something on the top of it like, and I can see her from the back as she leans in and like, oh man, it was like, it was like I was turning on fire inside me or something, it was like this volcano started up inside me, and I don't think, I mean, I know I'd never been so turned on before, it was like *Whoa!* And—what, did I get wood? Of course I got fuckin' wood, what are you kiddin' me? A fuckin' dead man would'a got wood looking at that, it was like it was fuckin' *painful,* the wood I got then, it was like there was no intermediate time, like one second it was like just there all soft and shit and forgotten, and like one second later *boing* like cement and I thought of those car commercials for fast cars where they go from like zero to sixty in one second, like no in-between time. You know what I mean? But like I couldn't do nothin' with it because it was in my pants, and I had to keep playin', it was like the best I'd ever played that night somehow, like all spontaneous and shit but the best I ever played, it was like I was their soundtrack, you know? And so this girl is like leaning into the mirror and she's like got this beautiful body, flawless, like all smooth and soft, and she's doing something in the mirror, and then I just shift a little over and I can see she's like putting on lipstick, and then she's like doing that thing women do after they put on lipstick, like puckering her lips like *mmp mmmp*—you know what I mean? And I felt my dick just like leap up when she did that, not just at what she was doing but like what was gonna happen. You know? And then like the guy comes back and he's got a glass of water, and he walks down the hall and into the room and he's got like major wood too, his dick's like swinging back and forth and pointing up as he's walking—I dunno, maybe they were like twenty, twenty-three, something like that, a couple of years younger than me at the time I guess—well yeah, he had a nice body too I guess, you know he looked fit, strong, whatever—and then he sees the girl putting the lipstick on in the mirror, and he grabs her again, and they start laughing and kind of almost like wrestling a little, and then the girl like takes the lipstick and slashes at the guy, and he backs up but she gets him and puts this big streak like on his arm laughin' and he like looks down at it and laughin' too and trying to rub it off, and then she starts again and pretty soon they're like each grabbing the lipstick away from each other and when they get it, like mark the other one's body with it, and then they kinda slow down a little and stand still and the guy's got the lipstick now and he's like outlining her nipples with it, he's like holding onto one of her breasts with one hand and like making a big red circle around her nipple with the lipstick with the other hand, and she's like looking down and laughing, and then she looks up at him with these big eyes, and then she takes the lipstick from him and they're both standing really still and she outlines his nipples with it, these big red bulls-eyes, and I'm going wild watching this and I'm still blowing to the music, like the three of us are in each other's heads and I'm the guy and I'm the girl and I'm myself and I'm the summer night and I'm the first time someone gets laid and the first time a kid beats off and the first wet dream and the hot summer's night and everything all unspooling like this ribbon of this this, like . . . *wildness.* You know what I mean? And then they come together and start rubbing their bodies against each other, like sliding their bodies up

and down back and forth and then they pull back and see how they've
smeared each other's lipstick like, and then the fire inside me just like
blows up and something's comin' and I feel like I'm going to faint and
for the first time in my life I shoot off without even touching it, it's
like blinding it's so intense and I hit this high note on my sax and everything goes black and for one second, like just one second I go to
this unbelievable place where like everything meets, the center of the
fuckin' universe or something and there's no way I can describe it, but
I felt like Superman when he was flying and all my life, this is the
place I'd wanted to go to with my music. Even Mr. McGreevey didn't
complain.

I started waitin' for them after that. I wouldn't walk down that
part of the street anymore because I didn't want to know who they
were, didn't want to see them by day. The next night I was out with
Denise and the night after that I was so tired from work I fell asleep
on the couch watching the Sox game and woke up in my work clothes
and it was time to go to work again, which I hate when that happens,
it feels like you're pulling a double when that happens, no? That ever
happen to you? But then the next night I'm like thinkin' about it all
day at work, *Hey Lughead, wake up!* I hear about twenty times that day
and I guess they could tell I was kinda far away at work that day, you
know? So then that night I get home from work and take a shower,
take a nap, and by nine it's just getting dark and I go out on my fire
escape and there's this light in the sky, the sky is all on fire over there
and I figure, huh, that must be the West, I've lived here three
years and never knew that was the West over there, and I watch the
sunset and think how I've never watched a sunset in my life, and then
a few stars come out by and by and I'm looking at the stars, like really
lookin' at the stars for the first time in my life really and then I think
how this guy on TV one time, this professor or something was talking
about stars, I was like too lazy to look for the remote cuz that's usually
not my cup of tea and he was saying how like the nearest star was like
thirty-seven light-years away, and the farthest ones are like millions of
light-years away. Alpha Centauri it's called, that star, the closest star
Alpha Centauri, I remembered the name because I used to go out
with this girl—we just had a few dates—this girl from the North

Shore and her father had a Alfa Romeo and she said one night the next time we went out she was gonna borrow the Alfa Romeo and we'd go out in it, but when she showed up she had some other car instead, like her car, this Toyota or something and if I remember right that was our last date, but I was sitting on the fire escape, this beautiful night, and looking at the stars and I got to thinking how, if these stars are like shitloads of light-years away, then it took shitloads of light-years for the light from them to get to me so I could see them, and how like they might not even be there anymore, some of them might have exploded or burned out like ten thousand years ago and they're not even there now, but we won't see that happening until the light from them gets to us. So the sky is like this big time tunnel—remember that time tunnel show on TV at all?—and I can't explain how I felt after that but it was like everything changed after that and somehow I felt like all . . . connected to shit in the world. You know? Like maybe I belonged here? You know what I mean? Like what a miracle life is? Like if the world could manage something as crazy and intense as that, then I was meant to be here.

No, they never showed up that next night, that guy and the girl there. But it was like it almost didn't matter, soon as I'd step out on the fire escape now I'd get all turned on, instant wood. Crazy, huh? I fell asleep out there, woke up about four, went back to bed for one more hour—we get up early, start at six, finish by three, which is the way I like it. And the next night neither. But then the night after that was Friday night, and me and Denise went out to the movies and when we came back, first thing we come into my place and I see that the light is on down the way in the window, and boom, instant wood and Denise laughs at me, points, *wow,* she says, *is that a banana in your pants or are you glad to see me.* It was almost embarrassing like getting a boner on the bus, not that Denise hadn't seen it before of course but it was like the boner wasn't really over her, you know what I mean? And then right away she took her clothes off and I took my clothes off and we did it, and I turned out the light but I put us on the other end of the bed so that every now and then I could look out the window raised up on my elbows and see that light on in the window, and I didn't even see anyone in the window but just the light itself being on was enough to make me crazy, and I closed my eyes and saw everything I'd seen a few nights earlier and when I came it was like crazy again, and when I opened my eyes Denise was staring at me like I was a stranger and the sweat was like dripping off my chin and falling down onto her body and she asked me if I had taken Viagra if you can fuckin' believe it.

I couldn't sleep too good that night cuz I kept thinking I was missing the show down the way, and my head was like kooky like with all these new thoughts, as soon as I'd think that I'd get hard again and Denise was like trying to fall asleep and she's like *what is your problem tonight?* And so I kept getting up like I had to pee and I'd go into the bathroom and leave the door open but the light off and try to arrange the bathroom medicine chest's mirror at such an angle that it looked out my window and down the way at the other house, and when I did that and seen the light on in the window I got so turned on that like five or six quick strokes and this big load came flying outta me again and all over the bathroom floor, which I had to wipe up so Denise wouldn't step in it if she got up to go to the bathroom in the middle of the night, which she did sometimes. So I shut the bathroom door real quiet and put the bathroom light on and then remembered the floor-cleaning shit was out in the kitchen, so I like snuck out into the kitchen and got the Ajax or whatever and then snuck back into the bathroom and shut the door and turned on the light again and then started cleaning the floor on my hands and knees with Ajax and a wet facecloth and then all of a sudden the door slides open—I guess I didn't click it tight—and the light from the bathroom goes right into Denise's face and she wakes up, squints, sits up, opens her eyes and there I am bare ass on my hands and knees scrubbing the bathroom floor and her mouth falls open and she gets all freaked, thinks I've gone nuts or something and two hours later we're still sitting on the edge of the bed, talking, you know how they like to talk shit out. But every time I think about the light being on I get hard again if you can believe it.

So that's like when things started getting a little rough with us, and then like I say the fall came and I hurt my back, and I'd still look out my window, yeah I'd still play my sax out on the fire escape once in a while but not as much cuz it was getting colder now, and sometimes I'd see them and sometimes I'd see just him and sometimes I'd see just her but it didn't really matter. And then things eventually got back to normal with me and Denise, but when Christmas came and I didn't get a diamond for like an engagement ring she got upset, she didn't say nothing, like I said, but she got pretty distant for a while, and then I started playing in the hack hockey league.

So anyways, after that night there when we played that Lenny's team with the dark Irish guy on it, that night and after that I kept thinking—*Jesus, how do I know him?* I'd lie in bed and stare at the funny ceiling and sometimes sleep at the other end of the bed and watch the faces on the train roll by, and sometimes I'd think I saw his face on the train, though I knew it was like just my imagination. So now like I had three things to think about, it was like I kept this treasure chest with me all the time now and I could feel it with me safe all day at work or coming home on the subway with my lunch bucket and I would think how tonight, tonight when I get home, I will open my treasure chest and take out these thoughts and run my fingers among them, like. You know what I mean? What were they? Oh, I guess I didn't say what the three thoughts were: the stars and all that stuff—I can't really explain how that made me feel—and the light in the window down the street, and then this dark Irish guy from floor hockey and how did I know him from.

And then, like two weeks later in the hack league—that was my name for it, the hack league—oh but wait, one thing I forgot to say about my treasure chest of thoughts—it was like, somehow, being connected to the stars—it was like the stars were the first, and then them two people, the guy and the girl down the street, and then the guy in the hockey league—it was like, by feeling connected to them, I started feeling more like connected to other stuff—crazy stuff, little stuff. Sitting on the subway going into work and the way the sunrise would like stab into the cars, lighting up the day and the people of the day, and before that I'd always just slump and half-sleep or worry about how long the day was going to be or read the Herald or whatever. A cloud, sailing over the Hancock Building one time at lunch, I just like watched this cloud just like sail, like this big white ship, and then I started thinking about how the world looked from that cloud, and how it seemed to me the cloud was like slowing down, to get a good long bye-bye look at the land below before it headed out onto the ocean, where it wouldn't see land again for four hundred miles or whatever it is to Europe. And that made me think of my grandmother—she came from Ireland. She'd sailed over from Ireland and now this cloud this particular day at work was like sailing back to Ireland, and I wondered if there were other clouds that were staying here that would miss this cloud. Weird I know, but this is how I started thinking, feeling connected and all, only way I can describe it. But my grandmother now, the story was, she came in from the fields one evening after haying all day, changed her shoes, and then walked five miles and got on the boat to America. With five bucks and the shoes she was wearing. And she never felt like inadequate or nothing for being poor, she always said she was rich on the inside and nothing, she said, nothing, could get to her or change her. But listen, if I had a nice apartment, and a truck, and a refrigerator and a couch and a couple of books and food in my refrigerator and stuff like that, which I did, why did I still feel poor sometimes? I'll tell you why, fuckin' idiot box. TV. It hit me then too, right at this same time, I turned on the tube one night when I came in from work like I always did automatically whenever I came home, you know, just to have the noise I guess—and then I was like ten minutes later, what the fuck am I watching this for when there's clouds to look at? And people to think about? And subways to ride? And I went outside and you know what, spring had happened while I was inside. I came outside half an hour after I had just come in and spring had happened, it was everywhere and I just wandered, wandered all the way into Boston Common and even the bus exhaust looked pink, even the skyscrapers seemed like just these big-ass birdhouses full up with chirpin' life. You know? And it hit me then quick how like TV is just work, more work an extension of work, you work your forty hours a week and then you work your second shift, which is watching TV so you can find out how poor you are and how you're supposed to live and what things you're supposed to go out and get, and then you work your third job on the weekends and nights, which is going out and getting all this shit that you were instructed to get on TV and when you try to explain to your partner when they talk about maybe saving up for a bigger place and you tell 'em it's too much work, more work, they just stare at you. Because Denise started starin' at me when I tried to explain why I didn't want to go shoppin' this one Sunday.

So anyways, the last game of the season in the hack league. All the games were on Tuesday nights, and there were like ten teams in the league and you played different times different weeks, like one week you might have the early game six-thirty and the next week the late game at ten and shit like that, and so the last game of the season we had the late game, and halfway through the game, I forget now who we were playing but we were kicking their ass and I just happened to turn around, it was like something you couldn't hear called me and I turned around right in the middle of the game and there was the dark Irish guy from that Lenny's team there, just sitting in the stands. Staring at me. He was in his uniform and it was kinda rumply, sweaty like, so I knew he'd already played his game and he was writing shit down so I think like he was scouting the teams, cuz the playoffs started the next week and I think they were a little scared of us cuz we'd given them such a good fight. You know? So I stared back and this time I know he nodded to me, just like this quick up nod of his head like. So I nodded back, I made sure this time I nodded back, and like I was *where the fuck do I know you from* because I did, I knew him, fuckin' realized it then, could'a probably started tellin' you shit about him, like, he tells wicked funny jokes, or maybe, oh yeah he has a scar on the inside of his left knee or his mother died when he was in seventh grade and he didn't talk for a month after that, I dunno, any kind of stuff. But at the same time I knew we'd never met really, you know? I know it's weird, but that's how it was. And then like all of a sudden BOOM, I get checked and go flying on my ass cuz I didn't see it comin' since I was starin' at Dark Irish, and right down I go and Sully yells *c'mon Lughead wake the fuck up* and I looked up again at Dark Irish and he had stood up, he was like . . . almost like a little nervous I got hurt almost, but then when I got right back up and started playing again I looked over again and he was laughing, not like at me but like with me kinda cuz it was funny that by staring at him and zoning out I'd gotten knocked on my ass and his fault kinda. But at the same time it was all too . . . I don't know, spooky almost. My mouth was wicked dry cuz this whole thing was a little spooky.

I couldn't wait like for the game to end, it seemed I'd look up at the clock at the end of the rink and it said there was ten minutes to play and then I'd look again five minutes later and it said there were twelve minutes to play. You know? Like school when you're a kid? ADD, they told me I had ADD, maybe that had something to do with it. So anyways, I was doing that because I knew at the end of the game we would talk. Me and Dark Irish. I knew we would. I knew he'd wait for me and we would talk and maybe he'd be able to gimme a clue as to like where the fuck I knew him from. Even though I hadn't really met him yet. Maybe, maybe I thought, he was at like a cousin's wedding when I was a kid and both of us both bored had hung out for a bit and talked about how boring weddings were? I dunno.

So like the game got over and then everybody started like congregating in the middle and talking and whatnot, and I felt I had to do this too for a bit anyway and everyone's like *let's get a beer* and people start talking about where they want to go blah blah blah and like slowly I turn, don't look up but like start walking over toward the stands, which you have to walk by anyway on the way to the locker room, and I'm like running my hands through my hair flinging the sweat out like and then I look up and the guy is like three feet away and he nods his head again at me like it's the most important thing he's ever done in his life and he's leaned forward, still in his uniform from his earlier game, leaned forward, his hands clasped in front of him, big white hockey hands. His notebook closed now beside him and he says *ah, pretty good game there,* and I say *thanks* and I stop right in front of him, because I didn't know what else to do.

Why didn't I ask him? You mean ask him where I knew him from? Because I'd been thinking about it all week, that's why, two weeks. You don't just blurt out with the Big Question first thing, you know what I mean? There's such a fuckin' thing as ahh, whatdyacallit, Diplomacy, my friend. That's the first fuckin' thing you learn on the streets of Southie. Then he started talking. To me.

I couldn't believe their defensemen didn't double-team you at the point after your first goal, he says. I had to think about that for a minute, I mean like I say he was like the brains of his team and he like saw all this shit.

Yeah, I know it, I said. I didn't know what else to say.

I guess I was staring at him, staring at him this close and trying to figure out where I knew him from, he had like this small mole buried in his right sideburn I happened to notice and Jesus Christ I was like *I know that too* because I did, I did.

You really exploited their nickel defense when they switched there after the second period, he says.

I could tell he was a really nice guy.

I know it, yeah, I said, though I wasn't really sure what he was talking about.

So I guess it's our two teams next week in the playoffs, he says.

Yeah, I said. *Yeah.*

Should be a good game, he says. We're still staring at each other and I could see Phil outta the corner of my eye coming in my direction so I knew it was time to go and I took a deep breath and heard myself say to him:

I hate it when people call me Lughead.

C'mon, let's go, Phil said, catching up to me. Me and Dark Irish were still staring at each other. And then me and Phil left.

You're awful quiet, Phil says when he dropped me off at my house.

I GOT MY LICENSE back that week. Monday afternoon when I got home from work my apartment was hot, it was end of spring now, May, right? So I took off all my clothes and flopped on the bed and I dreamed we were staring at each other after the game me and Dark Irish and in my dream I asked him *what's in the notebook* and I pointed, and he looked to the right, looked to the left, but everyone was somewhere else. You could hear their voices but they were at the other end of the rink, and he opened his notebook, tightened his lower lip and opened up the notebook, and it was like all these complicated equations like theorems or whatever having to do with floor hockey and the positioning of people, but in the margins of the notebook there

were all these quick sketches of me playing floor hockey. He started
turning the pages and the notebook got bigger until it turned into
this big art easel thing like, and the rustle of it as he turned each page,
like the flapping of very very very slow silent huge angel wings, and
with every page the theorems got fewer and fewer and the sketches of
me got bigger and more elaborate, and then they started turning into
sketches of other parts of my life, me Big Digging, me on the subway,
me on the edge of my bed on all fours naked with my bare ass in the
air looking out the window at the subway and all the people on the
subway were him showing me the same sketch that he was holding up
now, and then finally the last one, all in color and big like them paint-
ings I used to guard that summer when I worked at the museum before I got the roofin' job and it was me on the balcony playing my sax
with a boner and the light on in the window down the street, but the
important thing was that in that last picture there was also clouds in
the sky, Spring happening on stars light-years away, and himself sitting opposite me on the balcony sketching me playing my sax. With
or without a boner, I dunno.

I woke up and I'd shot a load, like I didn't even know it til I got up
and my dick was sticking to the comforter because it had like half
dried. First wet dream I'd had in ten years, like since I was fourteen or
whatever.

What the fuck, I said.

The room was so fuckin' hot.

I took a cold shower, got dressed, took the bus downtown and
came home with a brand new air conditioner. That was work, lemme
tell you, luggin' it up four flights.

I went out on the balcony that night and played, but my song was
sad. No lights came on and at ten-thirty Mr. McGreevey slammed
down his window and scared the shit outta me, cuz I guess I'd lost
track of the time like. My mind was elsewhere. Lughead and now this.
You know what I mean?

Tuesday after work I got my license back. At the registry this nice
black girl says no mo' partyin' now when you drivin' your ass 'round
town as she handed it to me and we both laughed and then I said, *did*

you see the clouds today? And then I got a little scared she would laugh at me but she said, *I know it, they're beautiful!*

Tuesday night I dreamed me and Dark Irish were talking after the game again and then all of a sudden it was very quiet and I turned around and all the other guys were standing behind us in a blocking semicircle, their arms crossed, listening and looking very pissed and I woke up wet again, but this time sweat, even though the AC was on ultra-cool.

Wednesday night I was out on the balcony playin' when the light came on five houses down. Course I did man, *boing* and my heart leapin' up like that. The guy walked through his door and off comes his shirt, tosses it, then for like the next half an hour he's walkin' back and forth, sometimes I'd see him, sometimes no, and he's talking on this little cell phone. Waving his hand up once in a while. Came to the window once, leaned out, flicked a butt out the window and listening to me play for a minute, then back in again. 'Bout half an hour later he walks down his little hall naked, ass going back and forth like that. It's funny how everyone's ass is different. His bathroom's right at the end of his hall and he leans over, turns on the water—was I hard? Man, I told you, soon's that light came on whenever it did I got hard, didn't matter who I saw or even if I didn't see nobody—like *whose* dogs? Pavlov? Are they on the West Side? What's so fuckin' funny?

All right, I will tell the story if you'd quit fuckin' interruptin'—

So where was I? Oh yeah, so he leans over, turns on the water in the shower, steps in—it's one of them clear curtains—and he starts taking a shower, kinda very weird watching someone else take a shower, like the order they do things in you know, and then he's like reaching up every now and again to somewhere I can't see to get shit, like shampoo, soap, whatever, and then this one time his hand comes down and he's got something in his hand, something I can't see, holds it up in front of him looking at it and then he starts like moving it across his chest like, his head tossed back, eyes closed, mouth open, and then he turns a little and I go *holy shit* and it's like the girl's not there but she musta left her lipstick there or he brought it in with him or something and he's drawn them circles around his nipples again, these lines down his body, and he's got wood and then he's slicking up his wood with it and playing with it and it's like I'm him, he's the music, I see it all again and *ahh* . . . we both *ahh* . . . like come at the same time and me not even touching myself again.

I can't look down there no more, I said to myself at three in the morning, still couldn't sleep. 'Fraid to sleep almost with the dreams I was having and Denise, *how come you haven't called all week?* on the answering machine.

Thursday night, beautiful night, I walk over to the garage there on Monk Street I rent, and took the tarp off my truck and went out for a ride. Just up and down the Boulevard. To tell you the truth I was so used to not driving I didn't really know where to go, but the whole time I'm thinking I'm like my boner now that first night I saw them in the window, like zero to sixty in zero seconds cuz my highs now are wicked high, connectedness and stars and Dark Irish and them down the street , but my lows are very low, Dark Irish and them down the street and dreams. You know what I mean?

Friday night Denise busted up with me. Yeah, hell-o, wicked surprise. I dunno, she was in a bad mood to start with, she'd got her hair cut and she thought they did a lousy job and it was all downhill from there. I even had flowers for her and everything. She said *you just been weird lately. You go to places in your head and you won't take me along.*

You're right, I said, I do and I don't take you along. What the heck, she was right. I had to admit that to her. She left halfway through the meal. *You never introduced me to your parents,* I told her when she was leaving. She didn't say anything but then she came back a minute later when I was sitting there slumped in the chair and people staring twirling my pasta with my fork and she said *That's cuz you're a Lughead.*

Yeah, it was a cheap shot, I thought. Fuckin' lousy haircut and you get a cheap shot like that. Was I brokenhearted? I was relieved, to tell you the truth. I'd have more time now to think about my treasure chest of thoughts, but yeah, I was very sad and scared too, it was like I had crawled out onto this iceberg and it was connected to the land, but now it'd broken off from the land and I was like drifting away from everything I'd known before. You know what I mean?

I picked up a few sixes on the way home. Took off my shirt and socks and shoes and went out on the balcony. Played my sax. Beautiful night. I don't know what happened. The last thing I remember is crying a little. When I woke up I was in the hospital. *What happened?* I asked. *You're all right now,* they told me. My hand was all bandaged up. *I didn't do this,* I said. *It wasn't me.*

The neighbors called, they told me. Heard me going crazy, smashing shit around. Took three cops to get me even with the blood pouring out of my wrist. Honest to God I don't remember doing it at all. The funny thing was, I felt really good when I woke up. Can't say why, but I did.

I wanna go to AA, I said, when they sent the shrink in to talk to me. Nice guy. Never wanted to put myself in a situation like that again, where I couldn't even remember trying to kill myself. We all agreed it was being so drunk, and Denise breaking up with me. I let it go at that. I knew there was more to it, it was this transition, like. Growing pains, whatever. That's why I have this job now, talking to kids like you who tried the same thing. Come a long way since then, man. And if I can. You know what I mean?

So anyways, when I get outta the hospital I was hoping no one would know, but word like that spreads, plus like I had the big scar and bandages on my wrist. I told people I got hurt at work, but then someone bumped into someone from work and they were like, *Oh no, he told us he had a accident at home.* Well, what can you do. They said I had to stay there for a week in the hospital. It was nice, they were all calling me by my name, Mark. They felt good. I felt good.

Good thing about having a union job, you get the bennies, and they have to take you back no matter what. But people stayed away from me after that. Except for this one black dude. He was cool, but everyone else was like *Oh yeah, how you doin'.* I bought these new work gloves that like went up past my wrists, started wearing long sleeves. They all stared though like they could still see it.

Tuesday night we had the play-off game against that Lenny's team, the team with Dark Irish on it. I drove up myself. I knew tonight I'd find out where we knew each other from. We'd talked already so I

knew I could ask him tonight, knew at least that question would be
answered.

Bad start for me. Like one minute into the game me and this other
guy were fighting over the puck in the corner and I got his stick right
over my eye. Naw, he didn't do it on purpose, we were just like mix-
ing it up in the corner and he caught me. I couldn't stop the bleeding
and the blood kept running into my eye. Blood stings, you know
that? When you get it in your eye? I couldn't play after that, cuz I
could hardly see. But like I had to, like I say we only had enough guys
to field a team and there's nobody extra like sittin' on the bench for us.
I mean, I stunk. Lousy on defense, didn't score any goals, and like it
seemed to spread to the whole team and we got our asses kicked.
Yeah, course Dark Irish was there, but I was so upset I couldn't even
look at him. After a while the guys started getting down on me, they
couldn't tell I'd cut myself cuz we wear these helmets, like lacrosse
helmets. *Lughead, what the FUCK!* they started saying when I'd miss a
man or something. I just started feelin worse and worse. And then like
still I was reelin' from the shock of what had happened to me last
week. It all started ganging up on me.

After the game my team didn't stick around. We all shook hands
with the other team, then they left. I'd finally stopped bleeding like
two minutes before the game ended. When it was my turn to shake
hands with Dark Irish I couldn't look at him, I was so ashamed of how
I played and everything.

Hey, he said, but I wouldn't look at him, we just shook hands. Then
he went back to his teammates, they were all like whooping and cele-
brating and everything.

I went up in the stands and just sat there for a while. I'm telling
you, I musta felt as bad as I did the night I slashed my wrist with the
steak knife. Not that I'd ever do that again, never, but I felt pretty
bad. I just wanted everyone to leave like.

Finally the place was empty. I got up and went into the locker
room to get my stuff. I took my shirt and helmet off and I had like
dried blood all running down my chest from the cut over my eye, so I
decided I'd take a shower. I took my clothes off and went into the
shower room there. Yellow tile, like ten shower spigots in there.

It took like ten freakin' minutes for the water to get hot, I kept stickin' my hand under but no, then finally. I washed the blood off my face and my chest, and it was like all watery-bloody running into the drain, and that kind of freaked me out cuz it made me remember how close I'd come the week before and me not even knowing or remembering. I really felt like crying, all the shit that had happened the week before and then me playing so lousy and always, always all my life that was the one thing I could always count on from myself, that I could kick ass in sports. Not that good in too much else, I guess, but I could always kick ass in sports.

And I hadn't cried since after Dad's funeral when I was a kid.

Then all of a sudden I heard, *Hey.*

I froze up. My head was down a little and all watery.

Hey, louder this time.

I turned. It was Dark Irish. He was standing at the edge of the shower room. He just had a towel wrapped around him. He had a great build, lean and muscley, not like a big gym guy but all lean and muscley like. I couldn't believe he was there, but yet I could. You know what I mean?

What happened? he asked. He could see the cut over my eye, and I guess the hot water had made it start bleeding again a little.

I couldn't say anything. I was staring at him. I gulped and it hurt. Blinkin' fast to keep the shower water and blood out of my eyes. He set his thin lips again the way he did—it seemed like he'd do this when he had something brave or hard to do. He took his towel off and stepped toward me. He took the corner of his towel and wet it under the water, then he stood right in front of me. Our faces were so close. He started dabbing the blood off my face.

So that's what happened, he said. *I was wondering. You do this right at the beginning of the game?*

All I could do was nod, like yes, yes.

Oh, he said. *I knew something musta happened.*

His voice was so tender. I started sobbing. I couldn't help it, it had to come out like. Big and echo-y in the shower room and all. Them kinda sobs that hurt? You know them?

Oh no, he said, lifting up my wrist and looking at it. Course I had to take the bandage off it when I showered.

Oh no no, there's no need of that, he said.

Really sobbing now I was. Kinda embarrassing but I couldn't help it.

It's okay, he said. *It's okay now. Everything's okay.*

I really believed it when he said it. He made me believe it the way he said it. Like the Blessed Mother was sayin' it to me.

He wrapped his arms around me. No one ever hugged me like that. I felt. . . . I felt . . .

Were we both hard? Yeah, course, I'd gotten hard as soon as I saw him because he was in my treasure chest with the two in the window and the balcony and it was all automatic now like the light coming on. Then he got hard after I did. But it wasn't really about that, that was like incidental or beside the point or whatever.

It's okay now, he kept saying into my ear, holding me, kissing my ear so tender.

Boy, was I sobbing. Unbelievable. But now it felt good, wicked good. It's funny how just one person's hug can take away everything bad you ever heard about a thing.

We just stood there for so long, me still sobbing while he held me. When I started stopping he pulled his face back a little and we looked at each other. He wasn't sobbing but his eyes were kinda red-edged, he was holding back a little. He had a little of my blood on his face and shoulder and I thought of the lipstick again and I got even harder.

How do I know you? I asked him. *Where do I know you from?*

I didn't ever want him to let me go. Never been hugged like that. All slickity wet too and everything.

You don't know? he said. *I'll tell you in a little while. Think about it, Mark.*

When he said my name like that—like my name had always been Mark and no one had ever called me Lughead.

C'mon, he said, *c'mon,* leading me by the hand out of the shower room.

Where we goin'? I asked.

You live alone? he asked. *You live with your girlfriend?*

Yeah, I said. *No, we busted up. Yeah, I live alone.*

Good, he said. *Then let's go home; let's go to your home.*

He dried me off. Helped me with a fresh bandage on my wrist.

Jesus Christ, I said after that, watching him get dressed.

What?

I knew that too, I said, pointing. *How you always put your shirt on first when you're getting dressed. How you always put your shirt on first, even before your socks or underwear or anything when you're getting dressed. I knew that, I swear.*

He smiled. What a smile.

Course you did, he said.

He had a little training kit and he took some ointment out of it and a Band-Aid and put it on the cut on my forehead.

When we got out to the parking lot, we walked right over to his truck, this big black truck. I was laughing.

What's so funny? he said, laughing too.

I knew this was your truck, I said, patting the hood.

Course you did, he smiled. *I'll follow you.*

We got back to my place. I'd left the AC on so it was nice and cool. I was so nervous kinda I forgot to show him how that candy dish rattled on the empty shelf when the subway went by, and I used to show everybody that. Well, there'd be a time for that, later.

First thing he did was pull down the shade. I remembered that too, how he always did that. I used to forget half the time to do that and he'd laugh at me, I remembered that now too.

I got something for you, he said. He smiled. He reached into his back pants pocket and pulled out a Superman comic. It was all curled up like.

I know you like these, he said. *Sorry it got all curled up. I know you like to keep them fresh, like. In that box under your bed.*

I didn't even ask him how he knew, I knew I was about to find out, I could feel it comin' like.

We were standing in front of each other beside my bed. He took his shirt off, then he took mine off. Then he took my hands in his.

He smiled, and when he smiled like that it hit me, I finally remembered. My mouth opened a little.

I knew you'd think of it, he said. He could see it in my eyes that I remembered.

Our future, I said. *I know you from our future.*

He smiled, nodded.

It was true. In my head I could see like a big doorway, which was now, my life at this minute now, and some things you could see behind it like, and some things you could see in front of it. Stars light-years away, and clouds going over the ocean at night, and springs, lots and lots of springs.

The Golden Apples of the Sun

Water, shimmery when they were in it. Moons in it at night, many of them, bubbling across the pond's surface like floats—whereas by day there was just the one sun reflected.

"I like your socks," the nurse smiled at Charlie. Charlie looked at them. Yellow and brown argyle they were.

"Th-thanks."

"You can go in now."

"WELL THEN—how've you been?"

"Okay."

"It's been . . . what? Two weeks?" The Veterans Administration doctor shuffled through some papers on his gray metal desk, then looked up at Charlie with small black eyes.

"Three weeks."

"This is our second visit?"

"Third."

"Right, third. Okay." The doctor began scribbling with a noisy scratching pen. A clock clacked on the green wall behind Charlie.

"Ahh . . . okay. Shell shock? Nerves gone wrong, anxiety? Was that it?"

"Ahh, no. Ahh . . . amnesia."

"Right right right." The doctor snorted a laugh. "Hard to read my own writing." He squinted at some papers. "Well. Okay. Um . . . re-membering anymore? Since the last time?"

"Here and there. Not . . . not really. Maybe a little."

"Remember everything since you've been back?"

"Oh yeah." Charlie nodded, rubbed his chin.

"And your childhood? Everything before the war?"

This was the third time Charlie had answered this man's same questions. He nodded again.

"So it's just . . . what can't you remember, exactly?" The doctor leaned back in his chair. There was a loud squeak.

"My time on this one island."

"Uh-huh. Do you remember anything about the island?"

"Some things. I remember going to the island. I remember—"

This was hard to explain. *I remember colors. I remember greens and yellows, the way the light came through the jungle green and yellow. Dappled. Dappling. I remember Tyler's eyes, the light blue of them. I remember Tyler waving me on, into the jungle. We both had feathers in our hair. I don't know why.*

"The Golden Apples of the Sun," Charlie said.

"Excuse me?" the doctor leaned forward.

"It's a poem; it's a line from a poem," Charlie answered. "You . . . don't know it then."

"I'm afraid not."

"My grandfather . . . " Charlie shifted and this time it was his chair that squeaked. "He brought me up. My father died before I . . . when I was very young. Ma and me moved in with Grandpa. He was a longshoreman, my father's father. He'd been a schoolmaster in Ireland. He came over here because . . . he had to come over here, and the only work he could find was down at the docks."

"I see. So what you can't remember is—"

"Wait. He'd come home dirty at night and tired, exhausted. He was an old man doing a young man's work. He'd be blue from the cold in the winter, white from heat exhaustion in the summer. He'd take his bath and put on clean clothes, every night. Then take out his poetry book. It had a cracked leather binding, green. Like a moss green. He'd sit down at the kitchen table after supper and light a tallow candle, and read his poetry, out loud. He'd try to get Ma interested but she wasn't, not at all. The line I just said was from one of the poems he used to read. I don't remember it all, but it was about longing, about . . . I think it was about trying to find—"

"Do you remember leaving the island?" the doctor interrupted, stealing a glance at the clock over Charlie's shoulder.

"Ahh . . . no."

"And from that island you went to . . ."

"Okinawa."

"Oh. You didn't . . . you weren't hospitalized then? After the island?"

"No."

"So it's just . . . what island was it?"

"I don't think it had a name. We called it Two-Seven-Four-Two. Just a speck on the map that we had to officially occupy. "

"How many of you were there?"

"Seven at first. Then just two of us, after we advanced."

"So it's just your time on that island you're blacking out?"

"Yeah. Some of it I remember but . . . not that much."

"Uh-huh." The doctor scratched his nose with his pen.

"But what I do remember is getting more . . . it's getting stronger. More . . . vivid. The stuff I do remember, I remember more of it, the . . . the colors of it."

"Are you working yet?"

The colors were everything, the colors and the Golden Apples of the Sun, and the doctor was skipping over them.

"No." *I can't work yet. I'm in this world more and more, this green-and-yellow world.*

"That might be a good thing for you, you know. I'm not sure amnesia is always bad. Something horrible must have happened to you there, or you saw something that just . . . you just don't want to remember, it was so bad. You see, we block out what we don't want to remember. It's what we call a defense mechanism." The doctor said the last two words slowly and loudly—just like the first two times Charlie had been here. He'd be telling him to move on next, to forget about the past.

"I think you should think about your future, concentrate on the future. Get a job, maybe get married. Look forward instead of backward." The doctor was avoiding Charlie's eyes and spinning a red pen in his thin yellow fingers.

Charlie shifted in his metal chair.

"What if it was something beautiful that happened?"

The doctor smiled and shut his eyes.

"I wouldn't think so," he said. He folded his hands upon his desk.

Charlie studied the highly waxed linoleum floor. It was seldom he felt like talking, and now, discouraged, the mood had passed.

"So . . . we'll say, another three weeks, McLeod?"

"It's McKenna."

"Oh! It is?" The doctor sat up with another chair squeak and did more paper shuffling. "Oh, right. My mistake; sorry. McKenna then. Say three weeks from today? Say ten-thirty?"

CHARLIE LIKED SITTING in the kitchen all night long. The dependability of the thing. Its utter uneventfulness. The old brass ceiling fan swirled ten feet overhead, making a chilly clink once every rotation. Sometimes he could isolate one blade, fluttering above him. From there it was nothing to imagine these were the copter's blades, and he and Tyler were being set down on the island again. This was especially true at sunrise, when the light that washed into the kitchen seemed vapory, tropical. Without even squinting he could see himself and Tyler, running through the jungle, feathers in their hair and mud caking their bodies; or sometimes just Tyler, standing ahead of him, turning around and waving him on, deeper into the jungle, into its slanting shafts of yellow-and-green light.

Tyler had discovered the pond on their third morning alone on the island. They had already fallen into a routine. Charlie would waken to a dreamland of calling birds and Tyler staring at him from across the tent, like a dog waiting.

"I'll be back terrectly, if it's jes the same to you," he'd say. Then he'd roll out of his cot wearing khaki boxers, put on his boots, grab a towel, and leave.

The third morning Tyler was gone for almost an hour. Charlie had gotten up, gone outside to relieve himself, then gone back to a half-sleep, still worn out from the terrors of New Guinea.

"There's this little ol' pond in the jungle," Tyler had said when he came back. Charlie opened one eye. He noticed Tyler's hair was wet and freshly combed, and his face cleanly shaven—

"Charlie? Charlie!"

His mother's voice swept away the vapory jungle air.

"Were you up again all night? You were up again all night, weren't you?"

He managed a smile as the dream figures fled into the chunky sunbeams.

"Will you please go to bed—please?" She made a noise of upsetment. He focused on her. She was wearing a white flannel nightgown with tiny red rosebuds on it. She hadn't tied up her battleship-gray hair yet; it flowed down beyond her back. Her wrinkled pink hands were folded across her stomach. Her gray eyes were stretched with worry. Charlie thought she looked like a squirrel sitting on a fence, poised for something calamitous.

"You're speaking tonight at the Gold Star Mothers' meeting, remember," she said.

He nodded.

"I'll make you some breakfast."

"Ma, thanks, but I'm not hungry. I . . . I made some eggs about four this morning."

"Oh. You can cook now?"

He rose up from the chair and put his hand on her shoulder.

"Don't worry, Ma," he said. He looked around the white and pink kitchen, trying to find something, anything, that wouldn't fill him with uneasiness. He shoved his hands into his pockets. "Ahh, I'm gonna take a walk. Down to the beach."

Her lifted eyebrows signaled disapproval.

"Did you call your uncle back? You know that's a fine job, a policeman. Though you could do better too."

"Ahh, not yet. I'll call him later." He made a move toward the hall—

"What would you like for dinner? A nice pork roast? A nice roast beef? I'm going down street later—"

"A-anything." He smiled.

"Well, what would you like? You were always fond of the pork roast. But if you're not sleeping nights, pork can lay heavy on the stom—"

"I'm sleeping fine, Ma. No, that sounds good."

"Which?"

"Ahh . . . wh-whatever you said."

"The pork roast?"

"Yeah. Yeah, that'd be fine."

He fled into his dark bedroom. He slid on a gray sweatshirt, then shut the white bedroom door behind him as he left. Closed doors confounded his mother, he knew, but she wouldn't question him about it.

He grabbed his brown leather bomber jacket from the front hall closet. Three empty hangers spangled onto the closet floor and putting them back seemed beyond him. He shut the closet door as if it contained a horror.

"I'll pick them up, Charlie," his mother called from the kitchen.

As he headed down the stairs of their second-floor flat, he heard his mother's pinched voice on the phone.

"He's speaking to the Gold Star Mothers tonight," she was telling someone. Charlie paused, as if he might get a clue as to who he was now.

"Last week he spoke at a fund-raiser for John McCormick," she went on, her voice rising. "That's what happens when you're a war hero. Everybody wants you. But, Betty . . . he has these . . . I don't know, *fits* now. Just sits and stares, and doesn't hear me. It's got me worried something fierce."

The front stairs were still steeped in morning shade when Charlie closed the front door behind him. It was like a dark pool of forgetfulness, or some part of the unlit sea, washing up to lap at his door. He didn't like it.

Then he marveled at how, before the war, right before, he'd passed down these stairs with a bat and glove slung over his shoulder, still a boy, seventeen and off to play ball down across from the beach. Only three years ago.

Everybody wants you.

He had counted exactly seventeen seconds after leaving the front door when he heard a boom from across the street.

"There's my cousin, the war hero!"

Charlie turned and squinted into the sun, splintering it above the triple-deckers. Franky Duggan was only his second cousin, by marriage, but the spreading fibrous feelers of cousins and second cousins, third cousins removed so many times from a great uncle on Aunt Hannah's side, were intricately charted, and honored, in town. Franky came trotting across the street, then feigned a few jabs to Charlie's wide shoulders, like they were boxing. Charlie laughed at this involuntarily. Even greetings between related men had to be draped in a facade of aggression.

"Where you been hiding, stranger?" Franky asked, clapping him on the back. "I never see you down the Club. Hey, looks like you're putting on some weight again. What are you tippin' the scales at now? Oh listen, we're putting together a spring league down at the Point, mostly vets. You interested?" Charlie opened his mouth but Franky fired off, "Oh, Sis wants to know when you're going to take her to a show or something." Charlie noticed how the morning sun lit up Franky's black hair, wet and spicey—fragrant with tonic. He wondered why he would notice this. He kept looking and saw the thick individual combed shafts, how they gleamed in the sun, each one as perfect and defined as the follicle enlargements from a magazine's hair cream ad. Tyler's face rose up before him, his blond hair fragrant and swollen with tonic—

"Charlie?"

"Ahh . . . " *Remember the hair, the smell of the hair tonic, that's a new memory now—*

"Hey, you workin' yet? Big hero like you must have a thousand offers, right? But lookit, we're desperate for men over at the car barn." Franky drove a bus from Forest Hills to Downtown and back, ten times a day. Riding all day and getting nowhere, Charlie thought. "They're even taking non-vets. The pay's swell, Charlie, so think about it, okay? Gotta run!"

"See ya, Franky," Charlie muttered, but by the time he had done everything necessary to say these words, Franky was out of earshot.

Desperate for men.

CHARLIE TEETERED at the edge of the Boulevard, three blocks and two unmemorable conversations later. A ship-long silver Buick slowed down to let him cross, then honked twice and pulled over. The back window slid down in jerks.

"Charlie!"

A smiling, white-haired red face emerged from the back seat's shadowy interior. Cigar smoke puffed out around the face, then vanished as the tang of the sea breeze sliced it away.

"Hey, Congressman," Charlie said. He shook the out-thrust glad hand, then shoved his hands into his pants pockets. His fingers found the ring. Each time he did this it was a shock. He knew it was always with him; but when he unexpectedly felt it, it never failed to freeze him. *Ma, this isn't my ring, is it? I didn't have this before the war, did I? It wasn't Dad's or anything, was it?*

No, Charlie . . . whose is it? It's a man's ring, I can tell you that. . . . What would you be doing with a man's ring? Whose is it, Charlie? Don't you know?

I'm not sure, Ma.

Oh, Charlie! Oh . . .

For a moment all he saw was a jabbering mouth and a gesticulating, cigar-laden hand, fading into a tropic sunset. He struggled to drag himself back to this nothingness.

"Congressman nuthin', kid. Call me Dan. Listen, Charlie, we're all proud, real proud of you for what you did over there. You gave a good accountin' of yourself."

Charlie smiled; there was nothing else to do.

"Hey, you ever think of runnin' for office? You know Joe Shea, the Lord be good to him, his old seat's gonna be wide open this fall for the state senate. Wide open, and a young war hero like you could waltz in. Charlie, you could waltz in. Christ, he could waltz in, couldn't he Pinky?" This was directed to the congressman's chauffeur, a chubby, balding redhead with small, nervous eyes.

"He could waltz in, sure," Pinky echoed, picking his teeth with his ringed baby finger and scanning the rearview mirror.

"Ahh . . . " Charlie shrugged. The sun bouncing off the ocean right across the street, the sound of the waves, the smell of it all, was pulling him away.

"You could waltz in," he heard again. "Call me, will ya? Will ya come and see me? Come and see me."

Charlie nodded as the Buick rolled off.

You could waltz in.

Desperate for men.

HE LIKED THE BEACH, more than liked it, knew it as home now. It was the only place he could go by day, if he went far enough down, without being bothered. Everyone was busy now after the war and had no time for the beach, except for the old raisin-skinned fishermen. Most of them were solitary and in their own world of the sea and its smell. But more than just the solitude, there was the sea all around, the sound, yes, the way the light was—but more than this, the feel of it, the closeness of it—the way it connected itself to every other part of the sea, every other piece of shore, even on the other side of the world. That had been Tyler's idea and it was so true, so inviolate, like a math formula. How landlocked Tyler had thought of it . . . well, that was Tyler. Charlie could close his eyes and it was like being back there, except for the gulls.

A few gulls screeched overhead. He felt no connection to them.

There were birds by the thousands on the island, but no gulls.

Charlie sat down on the sand, watching the sun splinter the white caps far out, where the sky and sun and sea become one glow—'Tyler Land,' Charlie called this luminous place on the horizon, blue and white and vague, where anything could happen. He pulled his knees up, grabbed onto them. Between here and the horizon lay a few islands, the Harbor Islands. Fresh hope jolted through him. Perhaps one of them looked like The Island, would seem more like The Island, and thus make him recall something of what had happened. He decided he'd go out there and explore. Soon.

The May morning sun was warm. There would be a chilly sea breeze later this afternoon—he'd be sleeping then—and the temperature would plunge ten to fifteen degrees in one hour. Ladies trudging up Broadway with their shopping in tow would walk head down, their noses reddening in the raw wind.

The weather on The Island was always changing, for it lay between the swirling trade winds moving the sky above, and the South Pacific current stirring the ocean below and around. But the temperature was always between eighty and eighty-five, even at night. Perfect.

The Island was in the shape of a teardrop (sideways), as if something were crying for what The Island had become after the shelling. The Island was surrounded by pink-and-lime-colored coral, which made it accessible only by plane or copter. From the air The Island was a series of rings: the pink coral; the turquoise water; the white beach; the neon-green slopes; and the innermost circle, the jungle hilltop, crowded with palm and coconut trees. The beach was pock-marked with craters, the only damage the bombs could really do to the sand, but the rest of The Island was scarred with barren slopes and catastrophes of tangled, rotting foliage where the fires that followed any shelling had run through the hitherto uncivilized vegetation. One spot near the smooth crest of the hill, about the size of a football field, had escaped the shelling.

I should write this all down, Charlie thought, *everything I do remember.*

The gulls swooping overhead cried and Charlie thought of Tyler's eyes, soft blue. Big blue, and open and tender.

He laid down on the sand, stretching out. He opened his eyes and stared up at the sky. Cornflower blue, but too hard, too blazing. Not soft enough. Not tender. Benign, but not tender. Just blue with everything behind it. Its vastness made it nothing. Tyler's eyes were bigger.

He found himself tracing his finger beside him in the sand. He turned his head, and saw that he'd started to write HONOR. He finished the word. Then he rolled over onto his stomach and wrote a few more words beneath the first. TRUTH. COURAGE. FAITHFULNESS. SEMPER FIDELIS.

Some of the guys in town had joined the Marines because of the Corps' reputation, its physical toughness, the well-known rigors of basic training. Charlie was more attracted—he'd told no one this—to a kind of spiritual toughness, a moral asceticism. It had always been this way with him. *My strength is as the strength of ten, because my heart is pure,* the words of Sir Galahad, was his favorite line from childhood literature, something that had become a mantra. He joined the altar boys at Gate of Heaven Church looking for the same sort of thing. He'd taken up smoking and made it profuse the summer he was sixteen, only so he could give it up the following Lent. He looked for such challenges, longed to writhe for a noble cause. If the causes seemed few and far between, that made his quest more sacred.

He had fallen in love with the moral code of the Corps, its demand for Honor, Truth, Loyalty, Integrity, Sacrifice. Boot camp was nothing; he kept his heart on his ideal.

Tyler had his own honor. This hadn't been apparent at first. Charlie had been shocked to discover Tyler had little respect for the Corps, for any kind of structure.

"I jes joined up to get the hell out o' Stimpson," he said matter-of-factly when Charlie, looking for a soul mate, first questioned him about it on New Guinea. He had avoided Tyler after that until they pulled the same detail on The Island. Then, they had been the only two left behind when the front advanced.

In the heart of his amnesia—which Charlie would peer into many times a day, and see about as far as if he were staring into an anvil—there seemed a disquiet, as if he had done some bad thing, or was failing now to do some required, vital nobleness. This was what made the amnesia intolerable, why he must know. Even if it was, as the doctor suggested, something utterly horrible. But how could it be any worse than what he'd seen on New Guinea? Okinawa? And God knew he'd never forget those sights, try as he might. The body pieces thick with worms, the way Jim Guinan's head imploded right next to him when they were under fire, and Jim about to say something—

But what if it was something sublime? Something too good for words?

He was on the verge, he felt. The several Island recollections were turning into color, and blooming, expanding, like The Island's dinner-plate jungle blossoms that would open at night, sticky with fragrance. Thick with insects, glorious things. Metallic blue dragonflies, foot-wide moths spangled like coleus plants—

He rose up from the sand. "Let me write everything down," he said aloud. The gulls screeched back.

He took the side streets on the way up to the stationer's on Broadway, where he bought a thick white notepad and a fountain pen. Bookish people, the smiling clerks didn't know him and gave him a moment's peace. The bag was crisp as the woman at the counter folded it over and handed it to him. Its crinkled crispness seemed pregnant with delight, possibility.

He passed the hardware store one block down from the stationer's. He stopped. *Turn back.* His conscious mind saw no reason for going back; but the colors did not live in the conscious part of his mind. He turned around, sauntered back, as if someone might be watching him. Patriotic bunting filled the corners of the hardware store's plate-glass windows, beneath which were displays of four different sizes of vaguely ominous standing hammers; a sheath of rakes; spring cleaning supplies; stacked cans of paint in a pyramid; garden fertilizer—

Paint—

"Charlie!" he heard from across Broadway, just as he ducked into the store, bells tinkling on the door as he closed it. The gray wooden floorboards creaked as he advanced to the farthest righthand aisle, over which a red sign with black lettering proclaimed PAINT DEPARTMENT. The sign was hanging from the ceiling on thick hemp string and it fluttered back and forth in the ceiling fan's breeze. He turned the aisle's corner with a racing heart. He took a deep breath like he was going into battle. Two large displays of paint samples, hundreds of them, lined the left aisle. The whites occupied the first rows, then these slid into off whites, then creams, then yellows—then yellows into greens—*yellows and greens*—

He reached for a sample card in the yellow-green row. It didn't matter that his large scarred fingers were trembling. Each gleaming white card contained five swatches of slightly varying color, laid out from top to bottom. Beneath each sample color was a number, then a name. His eyes riveted upon each one, one at a time—he couldn't rush this. His heart was pounding so strongly he could see his gray sweatshirt fluttering with each beat.

Number 3271 was Light Chartreuse. It was close, but just a little too yellow. The next one down—he had to bring his other hand up to stop his trembling now—was closer, and something sizzled inside him. The shelves grew vapory and Charlie could almost see, from the corner of his eye, Tyler at the end of the aisle, caked in mud, feathers in his blond hair, waving him on . . . but still it wasn't quite it.

The next sample down was too flat, not liquidy enough.

Number 3275, Whisper Green, was the identical color of the light that would filter through the jade and palm trees that formed a canopy forty feet above the jungle floor. The color glowed, vibrated, throbbed as Charlie studied it. A throb that he could see now ran through things, his heart, the pulsing of the moths as they sipped the flower nectar, the thing inside Tyler—

A bead of sweat rolled off his nose and fell onto his shaking right index finger. Tyler's face burst through the mist at the end of the aisle, more colorful than Charlie had remembered it before: the hair yellow as a sun in a child's crayoned drawing, the eyes robin's-egg blue, the smiling teeth flashing white, swirls of mud disguising, then blending with the white flesh, the feathers in Tyler's hair black and white, the olive boxer shorts barely staying up on the flat stomach, a ribbon of downy hair trickling down from the navel—but his face—his face, so happy, so joyous, what . . . what . . . he was beckoning to him from the end of the aisle, to follow, to come and join in something, to see something—

I followed him! I did; he waved to me and I came! We went . . . went farther into the jungle. We were playing this game, a game Tyler played as a kid. . . . We got to the pond. The light over the pond—the way it glowed—

"Charlie! Charlie!"

Someone was shaking him—

Tyler's face was more reluctant to flee this time. It faded in degrees until it became something else, some jowly head in front of him jabbering away.

"Tyler!" Charlie called, and he heard his voice break, but someone was still shaking him—

"CHARLIE! CHARLIE!"

"What!" Charlie screamed at the new face, and the eyes popped in front of him. Quickly it was Mr. Hogan, Denny Hogan's father. Charlie and Denny had played ball together for years and Mr. Hogan had never missed a game, as he always said.

"What's the matter with you?" Mr. Hogan cried back. His fat hands were still on Charlie's shoulders. "It's me, Charlie! Dan Hogan! What's the matter with you?"

Charlie noticed two or three shoppers and one clerk gathered at the aisle's end, where Tyler had just been, drawn by Charlie's outburst.

"M-Mr. Hogan," Charlie panted, his words threaded on a string of disappointment impossible to hide. He noticed the large invasive eyes, the swollen face, the trace of doughnut powder on the left side of Mr. Hogan's mouth.

"Yeah. Yeah," Mr. Hogan answered. He took his hands away, then hitched up his pants, sliding off his swollen belly. "Jeez—what are you doing, Charlie? Did I startle you or something?" Mr. Hogan stared openly into Charlie's hands, at the paint samples. Charlie shoved them into his pants pocket.

"Yeah," he answered, gulping. "I was thinking about something. You . . . you shouldn't mind me, Mr. Hogan. I get in my own little world now. Sometimes." He paused, swallowed, then went on desperately, "I just remembered something I'd forgotten . . . Tyler. My friend Tyler. We were on this island together. The color, when we were in the jungle, the sun would come through—"

"No problem, son," Mr. Hogan smiled. He turned and glared at the onlookers until they looked away and shuffled off. He turned back to Charlie. He put a fatherly arm across Charlie's shoulder. Charlie felt himself stiffen.

"I heard about your amnesia," Mr. Hogan murmured confidentially, his tongue discovering, then licking away, the doughnut powder at the corner of his mouth. "So tell me what happened over there."

"Huh?"

"What kind of action did you see?" Mr. Hogan wet his bottom lip anxiously.

"Action?"

"A lot of the fellas my age that were in the Great War say what we went through in the trenches was worse than anything you guys faced. Much worse, ten times worse." Charlie could see the beginning of a snarl on Mr. Hogan's face.

Charlie turned away and faced the wall of samples again. The colors burst out at him like machine-gun fire. Not only the greens and yellows, the blues of Tyler's eyes in different jungle lights—but everything now. There was one the color of Tyler's skin by day, another the exact shade of Tyler's glimmering, lightly hairy flesh in the milky moonlight—the unsunburned flesh. A wave of heat washed over Charlie. He started shaking. Some vast fissure inside him began to expand. The blues, the greens, the pond at midnight, the water shimmering green in the liquidy moonlight, Tyler facing him up to his knees in the mirror water, staring, then both of them rolling together in the water, the moonlight dappling, changing the colors of Tyler's flesh, and then the reds leapt out at him, the roses and pinks, subtle changes in the side-by-side samples from lips to mouths to tongues to the blemish below Tyler's back, every color a memory with the bright pink moonlight of the jungle filtering down—

He remembered. He heard a sound and didn't realize at first that it was himself, gasping—

Mr. Hogan was tugging on the sleeve of Charlie's jacket.

"You got yourself a few medals, I seen it in the paper," Mr. Hogan was saying, almost sneering. He leaned in closer, his eyes glistening and carnivorous.

"I . . . I . . . ," Charlie panted.

"So what was it?" Mr. Hogan snarled. "Hand-to-hand combat? Like we had? Any bayonets involved?"

He came in closer still, his breath redolent with coffee and cigarettes. His eyeteeth were slightly pointed.

"How many Japs did you kill?" he demanded.

The West Broadway Academy
of Martial Arts

We'd been driving in Virginia for three hours (seemed like twenty), it was around midnight, and my sneakers were smelly. Sean had the heat on because the top was down and the vents were blowing on my Nikes, making them sweat. I squiggled around in the passenger seat to unstick my flesh and pulled a hard, crispy-cold french fry from under my right thigh. Just then this preacher or something from a Southern church came on the radio, talking about a conference that was coming up soon that he wanted everybody to go to. He said it was the Annual Conference on the Family, and if you went to it you'd find out how to raise your children so they wouldn't turn out to be homosexuals.

His voice was high and buzzy-whiney like an insect's, wicked intolerant too, so Sean mumbled, "Get lost, why don't you" and hit the seek button. But we couldn't get much on the radio except country music, which we'd never sat through before but decided we didn't like too much.

Unfortunately this minister guy or whoever he was must've been syndicated or something; we pulled him in again farther down the dial, but with a weaker signal. Now his voice was wavery as the signal bent and floated around the hills and hollows like he'd been drowned but was still talking through the water like a goldfish I saw once in a toilet bowl cleaner commercial, and I thought *we'll never make it, we were crazy for thinking this would work and, also, the world's too big, too goddamn big.*

I thought of Grandma Flynn's story, of how one of her cousins, this Tessie woman, decided to leave her tiny village on the west coast of

Ireland and come to America. Tessie got up at dawn, said good-bye, then began the big-ass walk that would take her to the train station twenty miles away. Her journey took her up the mountain that overshadowed their village, and when Tessie reached the top, she saw for the first time in her life a view that extended for mile after mile. *My soul to the Divil!* she exclaimed. *What a big and weary world it is!* Then she turned around and went back home and never left again.

But we couldn't stay; they would've killed us. Me, anyways.

A woman's voice came on next and said "After attending the Conference on the Family, I discovered there were some things I was doing that may have prevented my children from becoming heterosexual, as God intended all children to be. I am now a better mother after attending the Conference." The woman pronounced it "het-ro-sex-yule." I'm just saying how she said it. I think it's unfair to say that the Southern accent makes people sound stupid. I like accents. It shows people have strong character like. The new people coming into Southie got no accents—they sound like newscasters from Anytown, USA, except they pronounce their "R"s even more and they name their kids Noah and Madison and Zoey and look at us as if we're the aliens.

Then the woman's voice wavered as country music from somewhere else, running through the hills and hollows, sifted its way through the car's tinny speakers 'til it sounded like the soundtrack to the woman's voice. She had more to say.

"After attending the Conference on the Family, I also know now what to be on the lookout for as far as what my children are being told in school by their teachers" She didn't sound intolerant like the minister or whoever he was. She just sounded kind of like a zombie. Like a zombie and wicked sad. "In fact, some of us have just led a successful drive in our community to have several teachers, who were telling our children harmful things, removed."

I turned to look at Sean.

We'd been driving for twelve hours since leaving, hadn't stopped except for at a Burger King in Maryland, which you really couldn't count because we did the drive-through, and twice to pee Somewhere, and before that six-packs in New Jersey where Sean said to the crabby old saleslady watching *Hollywood Extra!* behind the counter, "Hallo, sweet thang" in a Southern accent because he figured after driving so far we must be "Away down South, no?" Sean always did suck at geography.

Headlights from a car heading back to where we just came from sliced across Sean's face and lit up his water-blue eyes and I could see they were red-edged and they looked hurt by what the woman and the mean minister said. I wanted to hold him and tell him these people didn't know what the fuck they were talking about—God is love and vice versa (which Sister Claire used to say, I didn't know for sure but I hoped it was true)—and I opened my mouth to say it but then a soot-draped oil truck roared by, and when it passed us ten seconds later and we could hear again (we were in this convertible), Sean opened his little round mouth and said, "Dick."

I started getting nervous.

"Ahh . . . what?" I asked.

"Dick."

Sean looked down at the radio's green light and yelled to the woman and the mean-ister and the country music wrapping around the hills and hollows, "Dick dick dick dick dick!"

Then he laughed and put his left foot up on the dashboard. His legs were short and he could do that while he was driving; he always did that. He rubbed his hairy, bare left leg casually. He was wearing shorts and sneakers with no socks like me, except Sean's sneakers didn't smell, like mine. His body and its functions were Perfect in Every Way. I thought so, anyway.

I got very nervous.

"Ahh . . ."

I TOOK OFF MY Red Sox baseball cap, ran my hands through my flattop, then put my cap back on. I nonchalantly checked my look in the vanity mirror on the visor in front of me to make sure I'd gotten it straight.

I turned to Sean.

"Ahh . . . .wh-what do you mean?" I said loud above the rushing dirty highway air. Sean's weren't the kind of words that you can just forget about.

Sean smiled and slowly turned his head to me.

"That's really what we're talking about here, Richie," he said, jerking his head toward the radio. He reached down between his legs and extracted his beer. He raised it to his mouth and took a long gulping swig. I watched a few drops streetlight-sparkle down his chin and plop onto his gray Tommy T-shirt, where they got instantly absorbed. Then he wiped his mouth and said, "All them religious nuts, you see 'em on cable. Those ladies wit the hussy hair and the guys wit the dyed bouffants and creep suits. 'Today's talk is about dick,' they should say, and the fat choir in the background wit the orange robes starts swaying and singing, 'Diiiick, diiiickk, oh lovely beautiful dick dick diiiiiick . . .'" Sean's voice got high and funny and he thrust one arm up into the night air of Virginia and waved it and back and forth, and I had to laugh.

Just then another toll booth appeared out of nowhere and we zoomed into the thing kinda too fast. We had to back up a speck. We were the only ones there at this hour and the skinny old attendant looked like a chicken with the top button of his khaki uniform shirt buttoned, and his eyes soured when he looked at our Massachusetts license plate. His name tag had *Vernon Spivey* written on it in swirly letters.

"Howdy, partner," Sean said.

"Two dollars and forty cents," the attendant replied. "Want a 'Merican flag?"

His eyebrow arched and he held up a stack of flag decals that he must've been giving away. He shuffled them with a brown-stained thumb as he stared at Sean.

"We're all set, Pops, thanks," Sean said. All the old-man talk around Southie's DAVs and VFWs, including Sean's father (a Vietnam vet), was what an asshole Bush was, cutting Veterans' benefits and sending troops off to kill and die for oil. Jimmy McAllister's brother had been sent home for beating up prisoners or something, and it said in the papers that when he questioned his superiors about this he was told *These Are Special Times So Don't Worry About It.*

"How's the stem of your bladder tonight, Vernon?" Sean asked politely as he took his change from the dude, and then we started laughing and took off before if and when there could be retorts.

"How come his name tag was like all calligraphied?" I asked as we roared off again.

"Dunno. Cuz Virginia is for lovers maybe. What a sour bastard! I thought people were supposed to be friendly down South, no?"

"I don't know," I said.

"Well, he smelled anyways. Did you get a whiff of him? Like a large Italian sub with everything on it. Probably hasn't had a bath since he was caught in The Flood, the old bastard.

After a minute Sean said, "See Richie, those ministers like sex and what it can do and they enjoy it, and they go around and they fuck whenever they want and stuff, they feel the Bible tells 'em it's okay— *go forth and multiply you all*—so they say it's a blessing. And it is. But I guess that ain't enough for them, cuz they're always worrying about other people and whether these other people might be enjoying dick too, and if they're people like them it's okay but if it's people that aren't like them it's not okay. It's *sin*. Big fat sin and your ass'll go to hell for it. Fuckin' assholes."

He took another swig of his beer but this time it didn't dribble down his chin and shirt.

"So see, in their dirty minds it's really all about dick, who gets it and who don't and who deserves it and who don't and who should use theirs and who shouldn't. 'Today's sermon is about dick,'" he imitated again in the high funny voice, "'and God agrees with us. He's on the holy lookout too for people who might be using it in an unapproved manner.'"

A billboard whizzed by for a furniture outlet coming up that said STEP ON UP INTO OUR BEAUTIFUL SHOWCASE OF ROOMS! It showed in the foreground a blonde lady and a dark-haired man hand-in-hand and one designer little blond boy and one designer little blonde girl, all of them from the back climbing up into a living room in the background that was all lit up with golden light like it was the Promised

Land. There were five poles with cups of light flooding down onto the billboard and thousands of white moths fluttered around them hysterically.

"See now that little lady," Sean said in his fake Southern accent, hiking his thumb back to the billboard which was gone now. "Why, she's allowed to have dick cuz she's one of us. And that fine young father is allowed to use his dick whenever he wants cuz he is like us too. Cain't you see the wedding bands on their fingers and the fine childrens the Lord done blessed them wit?" Then he snickered again but his eyes weren't laughing. "And not only that, but lookit all the fine thangs that open up to you when you er allowed to have dick. Nice new furniture, big-ass TV, and a minivan to do your shopping in, and neighbors that you know will keep an eye on your fine home when you travel, cuz they shore 'nuff keep an eye on it when you is home, just to make sure dick ain't being used inappropriately."

But I was thinking I was like the moths, fluttering uselessly around the light of Sean and it would all be for nothing, nothing again; he'd go back in a day or two or a week or a month.

I'd never heard him talk like this before and I didn't know what to do, so I put my feet back up on the dashboard. But then I could smell my sneakers again and I was afraid Sean would too so I put them back down on the floor and looked at them and how skinny my legs looked. I wondered if they looked just this skinny from Sean's angle so I flexed my legs and that made the muscles stand out a little and they didn't look so bad. I kept them that way even though it was uncomfortable.

About ten miles later it was wicked dark, so I relaxed my legs, but we couldn't see any stars because the sulfur light poles on each side of I-95 were too glaring, like bright-brown camera flashes going off in sequence every three seconds.

Sean said, "Richie, I betcha a lot of people throw out the baby wit the bathwater and don't . . . like or believe in God because these people are such hateful fuckin' assholes. You got a stick o' gum on ya, Richie?"

"Ahh, no. I gave you the last piece an hour ago there. At the toll booth?"

"Oh. Huh. Well anyways, it ain't that fuckin' complicated, this God stuff. But you got all these people talking and arguing and fightin' over it, and countries going to war over it cuz they're right and the other people are wrong. Like God would favor one people over another, or be reduced to being . . . a godamn dick cop. People do that, but not God. What good's a God who's not for everybody? You know what I think?"

Usually when Sean asked that question he didn't wait for an answer, but this time for once he did. You get on a highway and Drive Drive Drive, and everything changes. Except the scenery.

"You know what I think?" Sean said louder above the rushing air, which smelled like pines and water and truck exhaust now.

"Ahh, no, Seannie. What do you think?"

"I think everybody's been given a different piece of the puzzle like, and the only way we get to know God is if we all compare our pieces."

"We all?" I teased. I didn't know what else to say.

"We all," he repeated in his fake Southern accent. "But no, see, God is good. He throws us all the occasional bone." Then he reached his hand over and put it on my lap and squeezed through my cutoff sweats. My heart started racing and my mouth went dry with heat. Then Sean laughed, and put both hands back on the steering wheel. But later when it was my turn to drive in North Carolina and I was exhausted and my eyes were imploding, I reached over to Sean and did the same thing to him. But he brushed my hand away and mumbled, "Not in the mood right now," and that made me so crazy with self-doubt and desire that I was coke-awake in a second and drove all the way through North and South Carolina without a yawn while Sean snored lightly away above the rushing wind, all curled up in a ball that faced away from me with his hands tucked between his knees. Little *mmmphs* out of him once in a while. Right after we crossed the state line into Georgia, we came to a rise in the road and a long orange swipe lay across the sky to the east. I pulled over at a rest stop because there was something calamitous tugging at my insides. The rest stop was empty except for closed-up rest rooms and a big sign welcoming you to the State of Georgia, the Peachtree State and Birthplace of Ty Cobb and also this big double truck pulled over on the side there that had UNCLE CHARLEY written across its cab in big swirly letters. I started crying for Every Reason in the World, which is the opposite of No Particular Reason at All. Maybe not the opposite, now that I think about it.

Sean didn't open his eyes but he slid his hand over to mine and gripped it tight. I jumped cuz I thought he was sleeping. Then he pulled his hand back, wiped it across his hidden face, and brought it back to mine. It had a tear on it—one of his, I guess.

"How come?" he asked after a while, when I had just about stopped. His voice was syrupy, raw. I felt this closeness fall down onto us from the sodium-sulfur sky above, like an alien spaceship's tractor beam.

"Everything," I said. I sniffed my nose empty. "What about you? The cats?" (I'll explain later about the cats.)

"No," he said after a minute. He gave a little laugh. "Well, maybe a little." He paused again. "I guess mostly cuz . . . I don't know . . . this world. It's . . . gettin' mean, Richie."

I'd never heard his voice come out just like this before. All . . . tendery.

"Richie," he went on, and now his voice sounded quavery too, not frequency-quavery like the radio mean-ister, but real quavery which I'd never heard before either, even those times in court when he was in trouble. "Richie, you're the nicest . . . you're nothing but good. If there wasn't you in the world I don't know what I'd think. Your . . . face. I always see your face whenever I get in a jam. Just . . . smilin', the way you do."

I sat up straight, fixed my cap again, and for the first time found my voice with Sean, with anyone. "We can make our own world. That's . . . that's what I'm trying to do here. With . . . you." I waited a second for the thudding in my ears to slow down a little. It sounded like the marching of booted soldiers. "And it won't be mean."

A loud bird that I'd never heard before started gibbering from nearby woods behind the rest stop where they were about to build a Burger King and Mobil "On the Run" gas station; they already had the signs up. I thought there was something especially frantic in the bird's every third note.

"We can make our own world," I said to Sean again when he didn't say anything.

Sean squeezed my hand.

"Sure," he said. "Sure we can."

AFTER ANOTHER MINUTE he said, "I can drive now for a while, Richie, and you can sleep." There was this mist in the air and it was very warm and things smelled green and yellow, and Possibilities started rising with the day. I could feel them.

"Awright," I said, unbuckling my seat belt. Sean never wore his, but I pictured us getting into a car some years from now in Florida and telling him to buckle up. The sky in this vision was blue. Biggy blue and endless, with palm trees and Life at the edges. "But I gotta pee first."

"Okay," Sean said, closing his eyes and sliding back down in his seat.

While I peed I tried a few scenarios on him: thirtyish, a little paunchy, sales, grimacing on the way to his two o'clock when a little of the egg salad sub he's eating dribbles onto his tie at a stoplight, and how many times have I told him not to eat in the car before an appointment.

But for now we were in Georgia and Sean said, "But you know it's really simple, Richie, all o' this God stuff. Love one another. Feed the hungry. Clothe the naked, visit the sick. Or is it visit the prisons? I forget now. 'Member Richie when you bailed me out?"

I nodded and took a deep breath. Sean had been trying to straighten out his act for the umpteenth time two years ago and got a job downtown at Jordan's. They got bought out by Macy's but we all still called it Jordan's. They put him at the parking ticket validating table and he wore tight navy blue polyester pants and a white short-sleeve shirt with a blue tie, and a maroon colored suit jacket that didn't fit all that nicely and had permanent BO from some person beforehand. You only had to pay three bucks to park in the garage if you bought something at Jordan's, but Sean had to stamp your ticket; otherwise it was like eighteen bucks or something outrageous like

that. Sean said all these rich asshole businessmen and bitchy rich ladies would always sweep in and say they lost their receipt and try to
talk their way into Sean stamping their ticket so they could save fifteen bucks, but he never would. He took his job officially. Like I say,
he had a uniform and everything. He was trying so hard to straighten
out, we met for lunch a few times and all he did was feed the pigeons
and consult his watch to make sure he was back on time. I was so
proud of him. Anyways, one time this guy came in and told Sean he
lost his receipt "but stamp it anyway cuz I'm in a rush." Sean pointed
to the sign and said, "I can't stamp it unless I see a receipt that you
bought something in the store." The guy was wearing a rich suit and
had attitude and said, "Yeah, I can read too, but I told you I lost it and
I'm in a rush. So what part of 'stamp it now' don't you understand?"
Sean told the guy the part he didn't understand was how someone
could ask him to stamp it when the sign said oddviously that you had
to present your receipt to have your ticket stamped. (Sean always said
oddviously even though I told him tons of times it was *obviously,* and
now I said it that way too and sometimes forgot which was right.)

"Okay, how much do you want?" the guy snapped, throwing his
overcoat down on Sean's counter and pulling out his wallet. One of
the buttons on the guy's coat hit Sean's lip on the way down and it
hurt.

"What do you want, five dollars? Ten dollars?" the guy said, pulling out two greasy fives.

"I can't take that," Sean said, starting to laugh. The guy grabbed
his cashmere coat and looked around in rage.

They sold greeting cards right next to the ticket-validating place
and the guy said, "If I buy one of those cards can you stamp my
ticket?"

"I can," Sean said.

The guy grabbed any old card from the rack and paid for it. A
NIECE IS A SPECIAL PERSON, the card said. Then he came back and
threw the receipt at Sean.

"Okay, *now* you can stamp it," he said.

As soon as Sean stamped the guy's ticket, the guy took the card
he'd bought and tore it up right in Sean's face and the pieces fell onto

Sean's counter, some on his lap, like fake snow coming down. The guy snickered and stormed off and just before he went out the door Sean called after him, "You know, you need to get a new attitude."

The guy froze, then turned around.

"Who the *hell* are you to talk to *me* like that!" he snarled. I guess the guy couldn't get over it. He'd said he was in a rush but I guess he wasn't in that much of a rush cuz he came back to Sean and said, "Listen, I got an eighty-thousand dollar car out there! I'm thirty-three years old and I'm a millionaire! What are *you?*" and he kinda snorted as he looked Sean up and down.

"What am I? What am I?" Sean said, and he kinda smirked. "I'll tell you what I am. I'm the guy who wouldn't stamp your ticket until you followed the rules like everybody else. Isn't America a great country?"

The guy freaked out then and started sputtering.

"You're a *loser!*" he practically screamed. "And you always will be! You're a seven-dollar-an-hour *nothing!*"

"Not," Sean answered. "And you have an asshole haircut." (Sean told me later the guy had like ugly Hollywood-long hair, which is bad enough on an actor but looks way stupid on a professional. It's fine I guess if you're a freak or too smart to be bothered or in a rock band, but otherwise it looks kinda stupid, no?)

The guy could hardly get words out of his mouth then. He was like sputtering and gibbering, and finally he roared, "You want to step outside and say that?"

Sean really didn't want to. I mean, he was on the clock and everything. But what are you gonna do? You can't really back down where we're from, it's all they've left us. So Sean got up from his desk and walked over to the guy.

They stepped out through the revolving doors onto the street and the guy started talking to Sean and saying, "Hey. Wait, man, we can talk this out," and then all of a sudden he threw a wild, sneaky sucker punch. Sean ducked, then hit the guy once and decked him. Unfortunately a cop was across the street and, to make a long story short, this guy was like a big-shot lawyer and his uncle was a state rep or I forget a judge or something and then of course they found out Sean was on probation (nothing serious) so they brought him to The Place Where They Keep Poor People—jail. And of course he lost his job at Jordan's, so he just figgered there was no sense in trying to straighten out cuz the world really doesn't want you to. They say they do but then they put all these roadblocks up to make sure you stay in your seven-dollar-an-hour place.

So Sean went back to dealing coke to make his and his sister's rent—just a little, not too much, and he always made sure kids never got it—but word was getting out and the cops were cracking down now that the new people were moving in, and I guess now the streets were worth cleaning up. Plus, one of the social workers had really gotten to him down at the Community House and he'd been clean for a month now, attending meetings for a month now. But people were starting to find out about me. I'd been seen once or twice cruising down Carson Beach and the L Street Bathhouse and whatnot, and sooner or later somebody would've killed me. The priest in confession told me to think of it as a blessing, and Dad before he died said *We love you no matter what,* but nobody ever said that out on the streets.

The truth of it is me and Sean had been fooling around since we were sixteen (we were twenty-one now) even though Sean had tons of girlfriends. It all started when a bunch of us were hanging out one night and drinking and so forth, and we were talking about girls and then we decided to go down to the beach and watch the sun come up. And then a few guys went home, and then Fitzy passed out, and when the cops drove by the beach and sliced their headlights at us we bolted, and we all kinda got separated except for me and Sean. And then it started getting cold and we went way way down the beach behind the old pumping station and started falling asleep huddled next to each other, though my heart was going wild with Sean so close. And then Sean's hand wandered Down There even though he was pretending to be asleep. Then he kind of shifted so my hand was on top of him Down There, and that's how it was the first few times; he'd always pretend to be asleep. But then one time I got sick of his pretending so I told him this wicked funny joke while he was faking that he was asleep, and he started laughing and then wrestled the shit out of me because he was mad that I knew he was never sleeping.

"It's just these girls won't put out," he said. That was the next thing he'd always say. "I just close my eyes and pretend it's a girl."

I wanted to say, "Yeah, but girls don't have this, and you do things to it," but I didn't want to push it or stop what was going on. I was waiting for the right moment. Still waiting now, I guess.

I guess in my heart of hearts I was afraid Sean wasn't really like me—you know, like . . . like queer or whatever—and instead he was just shell-shocked or always horny or whatever, postmodern straight, which is why I was very surprised when I told him a month ago that people were starting to talk about me, and sooner or later someone would get me and beat the shit outta me or kill me, even, and so I had to leave Southie, and he said he'd go with me too as long as we went to Florida.

I still wasn't sure at all until this morning, when he picked me up in this white convertible a little after 11:00, Ma denouncing Sean and my plans as I threw everything into one big Ames plastic bag I found tucked on the downstairs railing. When I asked him whose ride this was, Sean said someone owed him a pile of money for coke and they gave him this car instead, which I really didn't believe, but I hadn't had the chance yet to rifle through the glove department (as Sean always called the glove compartment) to take a peek at the registration and see whose car this really was. I figured it must be somebody else's; Sean wouldn't be doing the speed limit otherwise, which he had been since we started this morning. I felt bad that it was probably someone else's car, probably some nice old lady's, based on the daisy ornament on top of the antenna, but, see, we just had this one chance, and I knew Sean would ditch it once we got to Florida. Plus, he'd been careful all the way down, even having the guy check the oil when we stopped for gas somewhere, maybe Delaware, I think. And then how he wiped up the ketchup that got smeared across my seat from the french fries. I mean, how many people would do that with a stolen car?

"They'll all know about you too now, now that you've left with me," I said to him in Quincy ten minutes after we left the old neighborhood. I was trying to draw him out. It was the ballsiest thing

I'd ever said to him. "You sure you don't wanna go back?" I just wanted to be sure of him.

Sean looked in the rearview mirror and you could still see a wobbly Southie there in the reflection and he mumbled, "It's already too late, Richie." He sounded scared. Most Valuable Player that one year in Little League, and now this.

I should've kept going and asked what I wanted to know more than anything: "Are we gonna try to make it together, me and you?" but I was afraid. See, Sean still tried to pick up girls. He was always chatting them up and flirting but I suspected sometimes he did it just cuz I was there, cuz he'd always look at me with those big blue eyes and a little smirk on his face after he'd do this. Girls really went for Sean.

Sean's license said he was 5'8" but I think that was exaggerating it a little, and his hands were small and white and his feet were small and white, but he was built like a brick shithouse, and when he opened his small round mouth this huge big bass voice came out. And he had a angel's face and a hairy white chest and other things besides, which was private between us. He was the runt of his family; all his brothers and even his sisters were bigger than him but they were all dead now except for his sisters Donna and Maureen, and his older brother Jimmy, who was a big-time cokehead even though he taught tai chi or jujitsu or something down at The West Broadway Academy of Martial Arts. Sometimes I get a little dyslexic and I always used to think that was a place where troubled couples went for counseling, and when I'd walk by I'd see people dressed in white bathrobes kicking the shit outta each other and I figured they were just encouraging these couples to fight it out and get it outta their systems like.

I'd known Sean since kindergarten when he waved me over to sit next to him, first day and the smell of sharpening pencils I still remember. The smile he had then, before that crowbar got him in the mouth after Debbie Morrison's post-prom party. He had character, I knew it when the circus came to town April vacation in sixth grade and their red and purple posters plastered all over town said they had a unicorn. Merlin, the World's Last Unicorn. But it got loose the day before the last show, and Sean found him half-starved a week later down behind Abernathy Textiles on the West Side. If you can believe it, it wasn't a unicorn at all but a goat with a rubber horn cemented to its head and the horn was half hanging off. Merlin was bloody from battering the chain link fence, trying to get the horn off. The goat just wanted to be himself. Sean ran into Amrhein's Restaurant round the corner and the hostess there called the police for him. But really she should've called Animal Rescue instead, cuz when the Boys in Blue came they shot the goat; they said they had to put it out of its misery. Sean said it went backward when they shot it, like a rope was yanking it from behind. Sean said one of the cops was laughing afterward when they put it in an orange plastic bag.

Sean was quiet for like two straight weeks then. Before I'd always assumed he was a tough kid and didn't care about anything, even though he was my best friend.

But ever since then I'd known better. Now that we were old, Sean liked dogs and hated cats except for the two he had, Prince and One-Eye, two alley cats he'd adopted two years ago, which we'd taken with us. They were in the backseat when Sean picked me up, the two of them sitting upright, wide-eyed as tourists, their bodies still but their heads swiveling like dashboard dolls. The adoption process had taken six months. It'd taken Sean six months to lure those cats inside from the trashy alley behind his house. They'd been skeletal, hissy-wild, but untold cracked saucers of milk and catnip mouses from Woolworth's had finally lured them inside Sean's apartment the first cold night of November two years back. That first night, every night after, they slept on either side of Sean, snuggled each side of his tight white waist. Sean told me later he'd stayed awake that whole first night, singing "Rocky Raccoon" to them, listening to their purr-snoring, watching their occasional ecstatic stretches and how their tails would just like jump up outta nowhere. "Happy Cat Boners," Sean called them, "because before this their lives had been a shit sandwich and now finally . . ." He said it was like winning something.

But now they were gone; they'd gotten free in Connecticut seven hours earlier when we stopped to pee.

That bothered me a little cuz I knew Sean loved those cats. I kinda couldn't believe it.

They sprang out of the backseat when we stopped to pee like this was the plan the whole time. They dashed into this spooky-quiet field of tall grass by the side of the highway, their green city eyes blazing out delight.

Sean had been peeing and called over his shoulder, "Shit! Jesus, Richie, where they going?"

"Maybe they gotta pee too," I said.

Sean stared into the grass but they'd already vanished. "Well . . ." he said. He scratched the back of his calf, then plucked a feather of grass and shoved it in his mouth. Then with a burst he went after them into the woods. But he came back five minutes later alone.

"It's like a fuckin' jungle in there," he said. Neither one of us had never really been in woods before. He booted at an empty squished twenty-ounce Mountain Dew Big Gulp. There were bramble scratches on his bare, hairy legs. "It's like fuckin' Alaska or something in there. We'll wait for five minutes and if they don't come back, they were meant to be free."

We waited forty-five minutes and Sean kept whistling and calling.

But they didn't come back.

"We're leaving now," Sean yelled out. The bushy field climbed a long, low hill and then went into these woods at the top that looked like they went on forever. The spaces between the trees seemed especially dark and huge, like each one was a passage to its own different world.

We got back into the car and Sean started her up. He raced the engine and put his little hands up to the sides of his little mouth. "Last call for Florida. I really mean it this time. Prince! One-Eye! Princey! . . . *Princey!*"

But they didn't come.

So we left.

Sean was quiet for a long time after and I think he was almost sniffling a little but he tried to hide it.

He didn't say nothing 'til we drove through New York City an hour later and he blurted, "I hate the fuckin' Yankees."

Then finally after a while later he mumbled, "Did you see their eyes, Richie, when they jumped outta the car? The cats' eyes?"

"I did. Yeah."

"They were shinin' like tigers," Sean said. He sighed. "Well . . . they never liked the heat anyways. The heat murdered them. They prob'ly would'a hated Florida."

"Prob'ly, yeah."

I felt kinda bad, but it was already late March and not too too cold, and I figgered if they could survive Southie they could make it in Connecticut, or anywhere else for that matter.

The next morning, saggy-eyed, twitchy, we slammed just like that into eight-lane, rush-hour traffic outside Atlanta. It seemed weird, us with hardly any sleep and drive-all-night BO, and everybody else crisp and glaring in their air-conditioned SUVs. I secretly wished for Sean to put the top up so they couldn't stare at us. But he didn't, he put his shades on isntead.

I got the feeling everybody around us could tell we were Jobless, like they all worked for Homeland Security and had a new device that read *Yankees on the Port Side. Faggots. Stolen Car. Bush Haters* on a LCD display on their Command Consoles.

But screw them I thought. It didn't matter. Later that night if all went well we'd be in Florida. We weren't afraid of hard work. We had enough to put down a first and a last on a little place. I had this particular picture somewhere in my bag and I could just see it hanging in the front hall when you first came home like. We might be okay.

"So fuckin' smooth," Sean said, tapping his fingers on the steering wheel. He always hated the bumper-to-bumper thing. "All these highway, Richie. The filter at the Curley Pool broke last year and they haven't fixed the fuckin' thing yet, but they'd never let a highway break down or get blocked. Not for a fuckin' minute."

"I know it," I agreed, looking away from a woman next to me peering down at us from a vast vehicle. At first I thought the model name of her car said *ESCALATE,* but when I looked closer the T was actually a D.

It must have been ten minutes later when we heard the sirens behind us. The radio was playing an ad for Peachtree West Dental Associates and the lady, who sounded like she was smiling like an idiot, was saying, *Your smile is the first thing people see. Don't take chances in today's competitive world—schedule a bleaching today!*

I waited for that moment of relief when you realize the sirens aren't coming for you. I kept waiting.

"Shit!" Sean hissed, his eyes jumbly in the rear view mirror. A voice coming over some kind of loudspeaker, trying to sound like God, boomed, *Massachusetts vehicle—pull your vehicle over now.*

I guess our car was stolen after all.

The staring really got going then as we slid over into the breakdown lane, smears of stares as the good people of the world inched by behind their frosted glass.

"Like a yo-yo," Sean said, throwing the car into park and shoving his right pinky into his mouth. "Like a fuckin' yo-yo, Richie. Yanked back again. I knew we should've got the fuckin' flag."

His eyes were animal-frantic. I think the world would've flooded if what I felt for him then burst out.

The Georgia State Police parked some distance behind us. Two of them got out and started trotting toward our car, one hand on their sides where their guns waited broodingly. I flipped my visor mirror up and away so I wouldn't see them. The speaker-voice sounded again. *Massachusetts vehicle, turn your vehicle off. Put the keys on the dashboard. Get out of the vehicle. Step away from the vehicle.*

"Please, what a bunch of assholes," Sean mumbled, still watching them in his rearview. "Look at 'em, Richie. They think they're a fuckin' swat team on TV. What'd they just get a new Mister Microphone or something?"

He closed his eyes and leaned his head on the steering wheel. He looked like he was about to freak.

I didn't care to look. But I could hear the padding of boots, the click and jiggle of their things as they get closer.

"Richie tell 'em you're a hitchhiker and you don't really know me," Sean murmured, his eyes still closed. "Promise me."

My heart ached for Sean, for the unloveliness that was about to come down. I felt like freaking too. But instead I straightened my hat, then turned to Sean and started telling him that wicked funny joke, the one I told him the night he was pretending to be asleep.

Terry-Love: One Good Thing

They got Sully right in front of Jolly Doughnuts when he was only like a hundred feet from his friggin' apartment. Probably less. Everybody said later, "What was it Sull, a black cop? Or some hard-ass? Or one o' them tough woman cops who always think they got somethin' to prove?"

As it turned out, it was none of them. See, Sully never told them *that* was his apartment two doors up. Duh. Because he hadn't changed the address on his license yet, it still said he was living in Cambridge. ('Member when he had that nasty apartment for two months with that Latino girl in Cambridge?) He thought he'd get into trouble for not updating his license, so he didn't say nothing. So they handcuffed him and busted his ass for DUI instead. When, if he had told them he was two driveways away from home, they probably would've let him go. Duh.

Sully could give you a headache when he went all philosophical and deep on you, picking at a plaster splotch on his drywalling pants while those baby blues got all faraway and dreamy. Earth to Sully. But when you got right down to it, he wasn't the brightest bulb in the circuit when it came to just plain two-and-two-makes-four common sense.

Fitzy they snagged in Brockton. He was coming home from a party and ended up in Brockton, though how you get from Hyde Park to Brockton when you're trying to get back to Southie is a mystery. The cops were laughing, watching him from a parking lot with their lights out. Fitzy sat through three green lights trying to light a cigarette and then they went over and grabbed him. When they asked him where he was going, Fitzy said "Home." They asked him where home was and he pointed up ahead and said, "Just up on West Seventh Street, where the fuck do you think?" Fitzy knew all the cops in Southie; his Uncle Eddie was one, so he could be franker with them than most people would. Fitzy said later "No wonder they didn't look familiar."

Paul—now, we never did find out where and how they got Paul. One of the rules of this place is that you can't talk about other people, or speculate on how they got here, if they haven't volunteered the info themselves. "Taking inventory," they call it. *We don't take inventory on others up here. Ever.* That was one of the first things they told us.

That being said, there were four of us in our little room, and three of us—me and Sully and Fitzy—were from Southie. So of course we're gonna talk just a little bit, not in a bad way or nothing, just speculating. And we kind of came to the conclusion that maybe Paul had killed somebody when it happened to him. See once or twice during "Open Discussion," which we had every Sunday night—there would be about twenty of us gathered in a circle in these metal card-table chairs that squeaked whenever you moved—someone said something that seemed to spark something in Paul. He straightened up quick and raised his hand and said, "I know it, when I was in Bil—" and then he'd clam up real quick and kind of stutter his way back to silence. So we figured he must have meant Billerica House of Correction. That's where they sent you when your DUI conviction also included manslaughter. And he never said nothing about, like, last year's World Series, or where he worked right before or anything like that, so we figured he'd been on ice for a couple of years. "A guest of the state," we called it back home. Paul wasn't from Southie but he was the fourth in our room: half-Irish, half-Italian, dark Irish or light Italian depending on which way the light was hitting him and what his mood was, and when each one of us first got here he stayed close by our side. He'd never say much but he stayed close by our side. See, when you first get here you're freaking out and wondering how the hell has my life devolved to the point where I'm in this place. You gotta face some mighty nasty music, and Paul would always stay close by our side, because he knew, he could smell it, I think, that when you're alone in this place during the first couple of weeks, one of the first things you think about is how to kill yourself maybe. Paul was a good-looking guy, darkish, about six foot, and he always wore long-sleeve shirts, I noticed, but once in the shower—they never wanted none of us to be alone for a minute, even after we'd been here for a while—I seen this jagged jumble of red and purple lines on his wrists, both of them, and I figured *Huh.*

We almost lost Sully one night. That's when I started telling them all about Terry, Terry Love, when Sully came back from the infirmary. You know, I just wanted Sully to know, and then eventually the others, about Something Good. Something . . . Saving. You needed something like that to make it in this place. One Good Thing, anything.

What happened with Sully was, I guess he snuck out and broke into the fuckin' infirmary here around two in the morning and got hold of some pills. Just like Sully. He was quiet too, like Paul, but in a different way. Sully was dirty blond and quiet with faraway eyes, whereas Paul was quiet with darting, anxious eyes and twisting hands that he'd crack the knuckles on every three minutes—I'd time it sometimes. Wherever he was Sully would just sit there, his arms folded across his chest, his light blue eyes a thousand miles away. "Sexy Eyes" all the girls used to call him back home when we were growing up. There was a Rod Stewart song out then by that name and we used to kid him. The ladies were all after him all the time then. Young and old, single and married. Even some of the angry young mothers when Sully had his paper route when he was fifteen for crying out loud. He got one of them pregnant as it turned out. He'd been showing up late for school every day for like two months because he'd been screwing the daylights out of a certain someone over on West Fourth Street, and she had the baby and passed it off as her husband's. We used to kid him all the time; he was seventeen and had a two-year-old son for cris'sake. He was wild then, always laughing, but then over the years, you know, he put on a few pounds from all the beers and got a little bit beefier, then lost a few of his front teeth in that brawl that night over at Debbie Morrison's graduation party. Before, you know, he kinda lived on that stuff, having all this action and all these girls. I mean, some people do; it's their whole life. Though even then Sully would get quiet and get that look in his eye sometimes. But now like I say he was a bit beefier and the missing teeth and all, and as a drywaller working for himself he didn't have no benefits like most of the rest of us. And of course being a candidate for being a Friend of Bill (also like the rest of us), well . . . that'll fuck you up and derail your life (if you ever had one) better than anything.

Anyways, getting back to that night, of course Sully had been extra quiet when he first got here, everyone is. Except for the Bad Boys that won't be broken no matter what, until they break themselves. I guess there's a gene somewhere, I call it the Rebellion for Its Own Sake Gene. In a way I hope they never find it, because if they do they'll flush it out and everyone will turn gray and we'll live in a world where no one ever disappoints their parents. That'd been in the Southie pool since day one, that gene, but me and Fitzy and Sully and Paul (even though Paul wasn't from Southie) had had it flushed out of us (if we ever had it). This place'll do that to you. It's not anything they do to you here really. They're all very nice, to tell the truth. It's just you see that you've ended up here, number one; and number two, you don't have the distractions of life that you do back in Southie—back anywhere I guess—that let you duck behind yourself. And your issues. Not a word we'd ever used in Southie, but after the first week we were all saying it. Issues. We all had Issues.

Anyways. It was our second week here when Sully did it. He must have done it awful quiet, because high-strung Paul's a wicked light sleeper, so many nights you'd roll over in the middle of the night and you'd see Paul, staring and spitting out the window, cracking his knuckles. But Sully snuck out the window and somehow broke into the infirmary across campus (as they like it call it here). He never really did tell us exactly how he did it. I wish I'd seen it though. It's always interesting when the animal comes out in any of us, especially people that are so quiet and dreamy-eyed like Sully. I don't mean like in the *Now It Can Be Told* or *True Cop Videos* violent intrusive feasting-on-each-other's-pain kind of interesting. I mean interesting like in, when that stuff inside us—that ancient and wild stuff that's usually self-controlled and self-contained and policed and frowned upon from day one—when that stuff pushes itself out and all you can do is watch, cuz you see it as your own. Interesting because we all have it. Most people forget they've ever had it, it's been squashed on so much. First by parents: *sit up straight, go to the bathroom here, not in your diaper, how come you got a F in English? Don't touch your body there! What did you do to that girl? You can't have the car for a freakin' month!* Then later in life by that most efficient cop of all, ourselves: *don't go screaming through the South Shore Mall, pushing over mannequins and ceiling-high displays of His and Her Leatherette Grooming Kits for no particular reason other than you want to, don't do that, don't think this, what will everyone say?* As long as no one gets physically hurt, it's interesting when that wild stuff finally gets out. Like one time in high school they dragged us all to this panel discussion in the auditorium where they had all these bearded experts, none of whom had ever lived in Southie, and they forced us to listen to their presentation, "The Triumph of Busing in the Boston School System." Halfway through it Danny Doherty stood up, turned his back on the panel up on the stage, dropped his pants, and bent over and bellowed out, "Shakespeare!" Why? Why did he say Shakespeare? That gene.

That guy Thoreau, they got some of his books in the library here, he said our preservation is in the wilderness, but I think our preservation is in our interior wilderness too. But like the one outside us, it's pretty endangered at this point.

But no one saw Sully when he tried to kill himself that night. One of the night wardens found him halfway between the infirmary and our dormitories, sitting up with his back against a tree. His arms hanging limp on the ground and palms up by his side. His eyes open like draining sewers. Fortunately it was September and not so cold yet. He was almost dead from the pills, but they pumped his stomach out and whatnot and three days later he was back in our room, quiet and nonchalant as ever. Like he'd gone to Atlantic City for a bus-trip gambling weekend. He'd left the three of us a note, if you can call it that. Just the word SORRY on the bathroom mirror, smeared in his own blood. He'd sliced his finger open with a razor blade to write it; we saw the Band-Aid. But other than that nothing had been said by any of us, and you didn't ask Sully questions—you had to wait for him to volunteer information. You'd get that look.

The worst part of it all was, we were all pretty much in the same boat as Sully.

It was the second night since Sully had been back with us, one hour before Lights Out. Usually that's Quiet Time, when you just hang in your room with your dorm mates or write letters back home. But none of us had anyone back home that really wanted to hear from us, so usually we'd just hang out or talk or chill or read or play cards. No TVs in this whole place if you can believe it, though they say the Director has one in her office. Just to keep up with the outside world, I suppose.

Something had to be said because Paul was biting his fingernails and Sully was sitting in a chair under the windows—all of which had bars on them now, thanks to his antics from five nights earlier—and Fitzy was lying on his bed facing the wall, breathing out depression in time to Paul's and Sully's desperation. Now that Sully had tried it, it felt like we were all fated to try it sooner or later. Unless something got changed, switched. Some rerouting of things.

I stood in the middle of the room for a second and felt like I'd scream. My own shit, and everyone else's. Thank God I had that One Good Thing to grip onto: Terry Love. Unbelievable how just the thought of that would calm me like the hand of God.

It hit me that I had to share it.

I gulped and closed my eyes and blurted "I got something to tell you all."

Paul jumped, and his head snapped up so quick I thought his neck might break. His eyes darted back and forth between mine and his half-bitten fingernails. Fitzy didn't move. He'd always wait, look around like a cat. Sully just stared, those eyes.

Things had gotten so bad no one even asked, "What?"

"I met someone last summer," I said.

The silence still, globs of it dripping down the walls.

"I met someone last summer," I repeated, and I hoped they didn't hear the quaver in my voice.

"You did?" Sully asked blandly, in his cracky little-kid voice. You'd think he was ten years old sometimes instead of twenty-whatever like the rest of us. (At twenty-seven, Paul was the Old Man of our room.)

He'd say that about anything, Sully, when you yanked him from his baby-blue world—you'd mumble "I gotta pee," and he'd ask from across the room, "You do?"

Fitzy was still facing the wall, but his head lifted a little.

"Yeah," I said. "Yeah. I did. Last summer."

I ran my tongue over my upper lip, and grabbed a metal chair behind me and slid it into the middle of the room.

Sully and Paul were both staring at me now. Paul sitting backwards in his chair, bouncing his knee desperately, Sully with his dreamy eyes.

"Who?" Paul mumbled. He shoved a finger back into his mouth.

I stared down at my bare feet before answering.

"This hottie. Fuckin' model material."

They all looked at me.

"So what happened?" Paul asked, cracking his knuckles.

"When?" Sully wanted to know.

"Last summer. When I was up at ahhh . . . Shady Oaks."

Now, Shady Oaks was the place you went to if you had three DUI arrests within three years, a one-month involuntary program. If you got busted again after that, you came here, for three months, and had to attend the AA meetings they had three times a day in the cafeteria down the hall. If you got busted *again* after you left this place, you'd never drive again and you'd do time. Long time.

"Shady Oaks?" Fitzy scoffed, half turning round. "When I was there there weren't no babes there. 'Cept for the fuckin' seventy-year-old cafeteria ladies. Those 'Lunch Bags.' 'Member, Sull, how we called them 'The Lunch Bags'?"

"Yeah," Sully said, long and drawn out, like he'd been defrauded.

"This one lived next door, on a farm," I said. I nodded my head at the truth of this.

I said it so low that I had everyone's attention now.

"Would come over a few mornings a week to work in the stables. 'Member them stables they had there? How everybody got assigned to working in the stables with the horses? Like one day a week?"

"Yeah," everybody said at once.

"You mean the barn up there on the hill there?" Sully asked.

"Yeah, the barn. Barn, stables, whatever."

Paul let go a deep breath and cracked his knuckles again.

"So what happened?" he asked. His knee-bouncing got faster. He was the oldest but also probably the strongest, all lean and wrangly muscle and those simmering eyes.

"What was her name?" Sully blurted, sitting up a little straighter.

I looked around at each of them, then paused and took a deep breath.

"Terry."

"Did you fuck her?" Fitzy asked, rolling over in the bed and propping his head up on his arm. Everyone held their breath.

"Did you ever," I said, slowly, looking around again, "did you ever just look at someone, and when your eyes meet . . . you just know? There's nothing that can stop what will happen?"

"Yeah, but did you fuck her? Did you fuck her in the barn?" Fitzy asked querulously.

"Let 'im tell the story, Fitz!" Sully laughed, smiling and showing his dimples and broken front teeth. First time we'd seen him smile since he got here.

"Yeah, but did you?" Paul asked. His right hand dropped down to the lap of his green plaid boxers.

I looked around again and held their eyes. They could tell I wasn't making this up.

"When it's like that," I said, locking eyes with each one of them for three seconds, "you make love, you don't just fuck. You make love. You . . . go to this other place."

"Okay, so did you *make love* in the barn?" Fitzy asked.

"In the barn?" I repeated, almost whispering. "Oh yeah. We made love in the barn. The horses staring quiet, their eyes liquidy, large. And out in the fields, behind the barn, the crickets all around like a choir in church with the lights out. And one night in the brook— remember that brook you drove over coming up the hill? And up against a tree outside my bedroom. And another time, in the kitchen in the middle of the night."

"You did it in the kitchen?" Sully asked.

Paul's slightly canine-looking teeth ran over his bottom lip.

"Jesus Christ," he muttered.

"Bullshit!" Fitzy groaned. "You never said nothin' about this."

I held up the palm of my hand 'til they shut up.

"There's certain ones," I said, "a certain one. Has it ever happened to you? Guys, we been through so much together, but can we talk about this? About . . . love?"

Paul held my eyes, then looked down and shoved a finger back in his mouth. I winced at the crack. Sully still stared. Fitzy wet his mouth and looked away.

"You don't talk about them is what I'm saying, not in the usual way. It's like . . . you don't know how to talk about them. They get you here, like most of them do"—I grabbed my cock and squeezed it through my white briefs—"but they get you more *here*."

I tapped the left side of my chest, slow.

"Right here," I said.

"What'd she look like?" Paul asked, dragging his chair in a little closer. It made a screeching noise on the floor.

"What the *fuck!*" Fitzy snarled, sitting up in his bed and putting his hands over his ears; he hated that sound.

"Uh," I moaned, closing my eyes and shaking my head. "Beautiful. *Beautiful.* You think you've seen, you think you've come to know every single way a woman can be beautiful—sexy or trampy or just plain gorgeous or sharp dresser or killer body, or little-girl prude or tease or whatever. You think you've seen it all, and there's nothing more you can learn about what turns you on."

I paused.

"And then . . ." I whispered, holding their eyes.

"Yeah?" Paul asked.

"What then?" Sully asked.

"Then you see someone like Terry."

Paul's knee-bouncing got faster. He gulped so loud I could hear it. Both his hands were on his lap now.

"Tell us," Sully said.

"Look at the boner Sully's got!" Fitzy laughed, pointing across the room at Sully in his chair.

"Yeah, well at least I ain't pullin' on mine under the sheets, Fitz!" Sully accused back, crossing his legs.

"Shut up, you guys. I wanna fuckin' hear this!" Paul complained.

I waited until it was quiet again. You could hear a monotone drone coming from the room beside us, and you knew the four guys next door there were talking about the Sobriety, the Sanity, that still seemed so far away from them God help us. A hopeful boat launched on desperate voices.

"It was the lips I noticed first," I said. "The . . . lips."

"Which ones?" Fitzy laughed. I turned and looked at him.

"Shut up, Fitz!" Sully cried.

I raised my right hand and extended my forefinger into the air.

"That was the first part of Terry I touched. And the first part of me she touched."

I started moving the forefinger out, out, slow, slow, right there, right there. I waved my finger back and forth slowly. In a crescent. I closed my eyes and a moan came out of me, remembering.

"What'd they look like?" Paul asked. Both his hands were on his lap now too and he was leaned forward.

"I'll tell you," I whispered. Their bodies leaned in. I could hear them breathing, especially Sully, his mouth open, he was a mouth-breather.

I closed my eyes and saw it all again. I answered slowly, saying each word like it was a strange jewel.

"Full. Moist. Soft. The mouth open a little. Like those pouty lips them foreign actresses have."

"Uh," Paul said, shifting in his chair.

"Pink," I said, "pinkish. And her warm breath spillin' out was full of the taste of . . . cinnamon."

"What'd she do?" Fitzy asked. "What did she do when you touched her there?"

My finger was still extended in the air.

"She shivered," I said. "She shivered, and her eyelids fluttered down. This sound came out of her—"

Fitzy made an exaggerated moaning-fuck sound—

"Not a moan," I said. "A sigh. An *ouff*. A . . . surrendering, like."

"A sigh?"

"A sigh I almost couldn't hear it was so soft. Like a very, very slight breeze going through the trees down at the beach on a humid August night. 'Member nights like that down at City Point Beach?"

"Did you kiss her? What was it like when you kissed her?" Paul asked.

"Tell us about when you fucked her in the kitchen," Fitzy said.

"No, the barn!" Sully yelled. "Wit them horses lookin'!"

I looked at them 'til they quieted down. Then I looked at my watch.

"That's all for tonight," I said.

"C'mon!" they all yelled. Paul gave his stiffy a backhanded shove, trying to keep it from worming out the hole in his boxers.

"It's almost lights out," I said.

"We won't interrupt no more!" Fitzy said.

"Just tell us about what it was like to kiss her!" Paul said.

"Tell us about her pussy!" Fitzy cried, but Sully picked up his *Big Book* of Alcoholics Anonymous and lofted it across the room at him.

"Her kiss," I said, and they all froze. Fitzy dropped the book he was about to hurl back at Sully. Paul wiped a bead of sweat off his bare neck. His veins were stuck out like rip cords.

"Uh," I said, shaking my head like I couldn't find the words.

"C'mon, Danny. Tell," Sully groaned.

I looked at them.

"You know how it is with most of them you kiss? You're thinking, 'okay, this is sweet, sweet, Jesus-sweet, but can I lower my hands to the ass? Can I lift one hand up now and brush it softly across the right tit? Or should I do it with my wrist, like it was on accident?' You know, you're kissing, but you're always thinking about the next thing you can do, what next you can get away with, no? You know how that is?"

"Yeah. Oh yeah!" they all said. Fitzy's hand crawled under his rumpled navy blue sheet. He raised one knee.

"Well, with Terry . . ."

I closed my eyes.

"Yeah?"

"With Terry it was like . . . Jesus, it was like the whole world went away. When our lips met for the first time. It was like . . . it was like you could stay that way forever. It was like you fell into a different planet, you fell through a hole in the ground and came to the center of the earth and you were still falling, wondering but not really caring when you were gonna land. Electricity. Like someone put one of them joke handshake-buzzer things up against your mouth, and clicked it on."

"Holy shit," Paul whispered.

"Lucky for you I wasn't up there then, Danny Boy," Sully said. "I would've stolen her from you!"

"Better lose that gut first, Sull-dog," Fitzy said.

"Shut up, you guys," Paul ordered.

They all turned back to me.

"Kissing Terry," I said. "So soft. So unbelievably soft. Moist. Tender and warm. Like your mouth was lowered onto rose petals, rose petals . . . rinsed in cinnamon. Her mouth always tasted like cinnamon. You weren't even thinking about what else you could get. Like, you didn't even own hands no more, almost like you didn't have a cock no more. There was lips, that was all. There was her mouth and nothing else. Nothing else in the whole freakin' world. And you just know you have to have this for the rest of your life. No matter what. And you know you'll do anything to get it, stop drinking, stop drugging, stop doing all the crazy shit we do, and make yourself worthy of someone like Terry."

"Lights out, gentlemen!"

Everyone but me jumped when the hard knuckley rap came on the door.

"Whew," Paul said, like he was waking from a dream. He looked around, then jumped up quick and trotted to the bathroom, his two hands pressed against his groin. Fitzy rolled back over to face the wall. Sully climbed right into his bottom bunk with all his clothes on, like he always did. In the morning all his clothes would be thrown on the floor; they seemed to come off one a time while he was sleeping.

The lights went out three minutes later. I think Fitzy had already cum. Next we heard Paul, trying to be quiet as his body writhed and tightened, but we could still hear that strange whimper bash out of him at the last minute, and my bunk on top of his was trembling. Sully didn't really care. When he came every night as soon as the lights were out, he moaned loud until all of us were throwing shit at him.

But tonight we all laughed when he did it. It was the first time any of us had laughed before we fell asleep since we'd been here, I think.

"You're gonna tell us more tomorrow, right Danny?" Paul murmured right before I fell asleep.

"I WANT TO TELL you about the first time I saw Terry," I began the next night. We'd all rushed through Activities an hour earlier to get to Quiet Time. Sully had even signed up for the after-dinner Jog Around the Park and we knew why.

"I thought you were gonna tell us about her pussy!" Fitzy whined.

"Shut up, Fitz," Paul said.

Our group had grown by two—Paul had invited two of the guys next door to listen in and asked, did I mind? What could I say? Their eyes were like the dead fishes' you'd see on ice at Foodmaster.

"I had duty in the stable barn that morning."

I closed my eyes and remembered.

"It was deep in May. Deep. I don't know the date or the day of the week or nothing like that."

I looked up and met their eyes.

"You know how you get."

They looked away, picked scabs if they had any. Paul cracked his knuckles.

"You . . . can't believe your life has come down to this, that you're in this kind of place. Anyway, like I say it was my day to be in the barn there. The day was one of them perfect ones that only come after a long nasty winter that you're sure'll never end. The apple trees were all mad with bloom—there was no place you could be and be away from their smell. The lilacs too. The sky was scrubbed denim blue and puffy white from the rains the night before. Big mother rains, lightning too. The sun was warm on my skin. A day like this, kinda makin' you think they'd never been such a thing as winter. Though it was still like . . . ahh . . . November in my heart."

I didn't have to look at them; they knew what I was talking about.

"I was kicking down fresh hay from the loft, right, with the idea I'd rake it into the stalls once I got it down there. They told me to put out enough hay for six horses, but how was I supposed to know how much hay a fucking horse'll eat, let alone six of the bastards. I figgered I'd just kick down a shitload, and they could be the judge. The hayloft door on the second floor was open, you know that opening they had there like a big-ass window. Nice view from there. Out into the hayfield. Down into the valley. Across, way across to these blue hills on the horizon. You could see a church steeple halfway between, and you start wondering about all them Other People. All the Other People that are normal and have nice lives and aren't . . . ahh . . . drunks. You start . . . wondering like, what your life might'a been like if you grew up in a place like this. With, like, a regular family and stuff. I stopped what I was doing and looked out at the view.

"This line of birds dipped and sang through the sky. I thought of the word *diphthong*. It might've been the first day of the world. But it meant nothing to me."

My eyes met Paul's. He looked down.

"I went back to my duty. For some reason I . . . I don't know, I almost started to choke up. Then . . . this thing, something . . . called to me. I don't know how else to explain it. I was staring down at my forkful of hay. I'd been working like a bastard, as if I could sweat all the crazy shit out of my mind by working my muscles to exhaustion."

"That must've taken about three minutes," Fitzy joked.

"Then I stopped. Just stopped. This feeling came over me, like a thrown bucket of water. I wasn't tired, I wasn't any desperater than I'd been the minute before. I just stopped. And this thing came over me. Something called to me from outside the hayloft. I paused before I turned my head, just to be sure, to really feel it. Then I raised my head and turned around.

"The sun was in my eyes coming up the valley, and it blinded me. I held my hand up to my head, squinting. It was like whatever was coming—and I swear to you on my mother's grave I could feel something coming—was coming out of the sun. I kept looking, squinting, my sweat stinging my eyes but I had to keep looking, and something did come out of the sun. A person. Someone. Coming across the fields. On horseback. Holding the reins with one hand, easy, casual like. Like the rest of us driving a car.

"It was Terry."

A shudder zipped through the room.

"I told you," Paul whispered to one of the guys from next door.

"Was she like dressed like a cowgirl? Like Madonna in that video there?" Sully asked. One of the guys from next door, Ed, laughed, but I knew Sully was serious. Fitzy glared at Ed until Ed mumbled, "Ahh, sorry."

"No," I said. "No no, nothing like that. Just jeans and a dungaree jacket. But . . . so soft, you wanted to touch them to make sure you weren't dreaming. The way they hugged the thighs so perfect. The same color as the sky, like Terry was riding the sky. Old brown cowboy boots. A flannel shirt, red and white and green, open a button or two at the neck. The skin where the shirt was open shining a little in the sun. This thin film of . . . not sweat. Moist skin. You wanted to smell it, lick it. And a baseball cap, from some feed store down in the valley.

"But she might have been the friggin' governor with a pardon for all of that. Terry . . . some people are like a ray of sunshine, wherever they go and whatever they do, they seem perfect there, no? Un . . . unquestionably right. You'd no more ask her where she learned to ride or what she was doing here than you'd ask a bird what it was doing singing in a tree.

"She came out of the sunlight and stopped about twenty yards from the barn. She was facing me. Our eyes met. I don't know why she stopped. She told me later but I didn't believe her."

"What'd she say?" Paul asked. His voice cracked and he cleared it, then took a drink of water from the bottle between his legs.

"Like I said last night . . . there's some people, you just look at them. And ahh . . . you know."

Someone gave a low whistle.

"We just stayed there for . . . I don't know. It could've been a minute, it could've been ten minutes. I'd opened my shirt and the sun was falling on my chest, lighting up my sweat.

"Hey,' she finally said. The voice cut into me, like a knife made out of feathers. My mother always said it was so rude to stare, but that's all we could do. Finally I just nodded. I opened my mouth, but nothing came out.

"The others came up then, some to clean out the barn and others to take the horses out. Terry was leading them. That's what she did. She came up three mornings a week and led the horse rides. She held my eyes until the last second. Then she nodded, and turned away quick like she'd made up her mind about something, and led the group across the fields, telling people what to do. But in this unbelievably friendly way. You know how so many of them treat us like dog shit. There was none of that with Terry. Just to have her look at you and smile was worth a month's worth of meetin's, you felt that better about yourself.

"I still couldn't move, couldn't even breathe. My whole life had just turned on a dime. I knew it. This thing lifted from my shoulders—didn't even know I'd been carrying it. I stared out into the valley. It was the same scene I'd looked at five minutes before, but . . . I didn't know what had happened to me until later, when little by little it started dawning on me."

"What?" Fitzy asked.

They'd put a semicircle of chairs in front of me and I locked eyes with each of them for a minute.

"It's the most important thing you can learn."

"So what happened? When did you finally hook up?" Paul asked, pausing for a minute from biting his fingernails.

"Well, I didn't see her again for almost a week. Can someone get me a drink o' water?"

Before I could finish the sentence four of them were handing me their bottles.

"Thanks. So you know, I started to think I might've dreamed her out of the sky blue sky. But the voice—I heard it, last thing before I closed my eyes at night. First thing in the morning, before I even woke up. *Hey.* That voice. The smile that went with it. The eyes, how our eyes locked. I didn't want to ask nobody in case they told me there was no one by that name who led the horse rides. You know how it is. You . . . you get a little crazy sometimes. But I didn't think I was *that* crazy. But then I was coming back from a meetin' one night. You know how they have the meetin's up there in the library eight o'clock every night? On the first floor? It'd been kinda cloudy all day and blah, just gray everywhere you looked. Especially inside yourself. The valley was in a fog all day—all you could see was that church steeple, rising out of the clouds like a needle. But then that night I was walking from the library to our dorms, and everything changed. The breeze picked up, but it got warmer. It blew the clouds and fog apart the way the streetsweepers clean up Broadway after the Saint Patrick's Parade. The moon came out like a silver spotlight. I decided I'd just walk around a little—they're not as tight with the rules up there as they are in this place.

"Now, do you guys remember the old railroad tracks up there?"

"No," Fitzy said.

"They were abandoned. I don't know if you ever saw them. They ran behind the buildings and down into the valley, they went over the river on a bridge, remember?"

"I remember the bridge," Paul said.

"Well, I was walking along, and I cut through these woods, all spangled with moonlight, then I came up on the tracks. You know I always liked railroad tracks, 'member, Fitz? They've always been a comfort to me so I just figured I'd walk them for a bit. The rails were still wet from the day's rain, and the moon hit them and turned them into two shining silver lines running off into the drippy trees and bushes and then infinity forever. There was wildflowers and weeds growing up in between the ties. I was thinking of all the people who had ridden trains on these tracks, what their lives had been like, what were the things they struggled with. What were the things that made them happy. What . . . what people like us did before we were given the God-given program."

"Mmmm," someone murmured.

"I kept walking, and before you knew it, I found myself up at the bridge, where the tracks go over the river. The moon was shining on the water. There was bullfrogs down there, bellowing like mad. You could hear the sound of the river thirty feet below, rushing and gurgling away, away. The water was way high after all the rain, the spring snowmelts, everything. I know it sounds weird, but I felt like that sound was trying to talk to me, like it was trying to give me the answers I'd been looking for for so long. But no matter how hard I listened, I couldn't figure out its language. Follow?

"I walked out onto the bridge a little way. I could see the shining water below me, between each tie, like knives flashing in a drawer. I sat down on the edge of the bridge. I let my feet dangle over the edge. All of a sudden I felt all grateful for my feet as I looked down at them, for all the places they'd taken me to over the years. The Little League games, the thousand walks up to Communion, my mother's funeral when I was a pallbearer. And lots o' wrong places too, but that wasn't their fault. The moon was shining silver right into the water, and bouncing up into my eyes. The water was swirling. It seemed so soft, so warm, that water. I kept staring into it. My palms started getting sweaty. I . . . I stood up—the water seemed so comforting—"

Sully cleared his throat—

"And then I heard this noise. Someone walking. I turned my head to the right. It was Terry, walking down the tracks, crossing the bridge. Drenched in moonlight. Her head was down, watching where she was going, so she didn't see me. I lost my breath again, like the first time. I wanted to say something so I wouldn't scare her. But nothing would come out again.

"When she was about twenty feet away, she just stopped. Her head lifted up, like an animal's, sniffing danger. Our eyes met. It was like she *sensed* me. I heard a little inrush of breath.

"You," she said.

"I nodded, so she wouldn't think I was the village idiot. We stood staring at each other. The moon so bright I could see her blush."

"What was she wearing?" Sully asked.

"Light chinos this time, and some old hiking boots. They were brown with red laces. And a T-shirt from some café down in the valley

that a friend of hers owned. The Moose Caboose. Funny what you remember in life, no? And a mustard-colored work jacket.

"'Excuse me,' she finally murmured. 'I hope I didn't scare you. I . . .
I walk here a lot at night. I'm looking for barns.'"

"Barns?" Fitzy said. "*Yeah, baby!* She liked getting it on in barns!
Yoo-hoo!"

"Barns? I asked her.

"'I make furniture,' she said. 'That's what I do. I make furniture
from the wood of old barns.'

"'What about the horses?' I asked.

"'That's volunteer work,' she said. 'I always loved horses. I don't
own any of my own yet, so that's how I stay close to them. Love
horses.'

"The blood was thumping in my ears. And then I realized, her
voice, it was the voice of the river. The same voice, but one of them
was singing and the other one was speaking, one going in and out of
the other. Follow?"

"Smoke another bone, baby!" Fitzy laughed, tugging at himself.
"So what happened? Did yez do it that night?"

"'So why you looking for barns?' I asked her. She had this way of
pausing before everything she said.

"'When I make my furniture, I like to use chestnut wood mostly,'
she said. 'But all the chestnut trees were wiped out a hundred years
ago by a disease.'

"'Oh,' I said. We both started walking toward each other a little.

"'The only place you can find chestnut wood now is in old fallen-
down barns,' she said, but her eyes staring into mine were like . . . ahh,
I dunno, like the water down at Castle Island causeway where it's all
deep and rushing. Rushy. It could drown you, like. 'Oh,' I said again.

"'The old barn builders used nothing else when they could find it.
Chestnut was the best. It lasts forever.'

"Her voice was a murmur now. We were close by then. Face to
face. I could see the moons in her eyes. I could smell her. She smelled
of . . . the woods, and outdoors, and the earth in the spring."

"And cinnamon," Paul said, turning to the guys from next door.
"Her breath always smelled like cinnamon."

"Yeah," I said, "that's right."

"'The tracks are a good place to walk because you can see a lot of old barns that you can't see from the road,' Terry said, and the whole world drained away when she talked.

"Then we just stared at each other. I felt like I was falling into her eyes. The longer we stared, the more we . . . the more we both knew. And then . . . and then . . ."

—I was shaking again just to remember it, the way it had been that night—

"And then she . . . reached out and touched me."

"Holy shit," Paul mumbled.

"Where?" Sully asked.

"On my lips," I said. I closed my eyes. "My lower lip. Her eyes never left mine. But she raised up her hand, slowly. This look came into her face that made my heart stop, like all the joy and all the sorrow of the world mixed together. What a chance she was taking. You can't understand. She extended her finger. I could see it out of the corner of my eye, coming in close. Coming, coming. She touched my lower lip, gentle like a snowflake falling onto another snowflake on somebody's windshield.

"'Is that okay?' she murmured.

"'Oh Jesus. Who . . . who are you' was all I could say, losing my breath.

"'Terry,' she said, but what I really meant was 'Where do you come from? Who are you? What the hell do you see in me?' You know, all the questions we ask when love, when anything good, finally comes our way. We just can't believe it, so we throw it away. But I knew this was too big for even me to throw away—"

"Lights out, gentlemen!"

Even I jumped this time. Ed looked up at the clock on the wall like he couldn't believe it was 10:00 already; none of us could.

"Fuck," Fitzy said.

"Tomorrow night?" The other guy from next door asked, getting up, arranging his stiff dick in his sweatpants.

"Tomorrow night," I said. I headed for the bathroom while Paul put the chairs away. Sully was going to hit the head too, but he stopped short when he saw me.

"You go first, bud," he said. Which wasn't really like him.

AFTER THE NOONTIME meeting the next day, I spent my one hour of Independent Study in a deserted corner of the library, reading *The Art of Tale-Telling* and *It Pays to Increase Your Vocabulary*. I picked a sunny corner. I just wanted to make sure I got the story right. I was only just beginning myself to realize the power of Terry Love. Amusement. Audacious. Auspicious. Adroit.

The last fifteen minutes of my free hour I wrote a letter to Terry.

> I'm telling them about you here. Telling them all about you. If you still feel the same way, if you really meant what you said, I'm getting out of here in a month. I've been thinking a lot about what you said. If you still mean what you said, let me know.

THERE WERE NINE in the room later that night. Fitzy wanted to charge a two-buck admission but Paul told him to forget about it. Fitzy made his bed before everyone showed up, and even took a shower and shaved. Sully came back from his jog with these orange-berried vines and stuck them in a glassful of water on one of the windowsills. Fitzy watched with amusement from his bed, but when he opened his mouth to make a wisecrack I gave him a look to keep him quiet. An audacious look, it was kinda audacious.

"Maybe they'd look better in that glass jar on the bookshelf instead o' that plastic cup, Sull," I said.

"They would?" Sully asked.

"WHERE WERE WE?" I asked.

"On the train tracks," Paul said instantly. His arms were crossed so tight and his knee bouncing so rapidly I thought he was in danger of losing his limbs at any minute. His limbs looked stiff and not at all adroit.

"I don't want to talk about that," I said.

That had been our first night together and the experience was still too . . . too something to talk about. Too hot, too raw. Too fiery. It had whacked me to my foundations. I was still hearing the echoes.

"Aw, *man!*" Fitzy's groan was the only one I could make out above the general tumult that followed. My hand, raised up slow, silenced them all.

"I'll tell you about the garden," I said.

"You did it in the garden?" Sully gasped.

"They did, you know," I heard Fitzy telling one of the neighbors lowly. "In the kitchen, too. They fuckin' did it everywhere."

"What's the difference," I said. "What's the difference between spring and summer? It can be just as hot in May as it is in August."

Nine squirming faces looked at mine.

"It's in the nights donchaknow," I said. "It's all in the nights. It's like three seasons out of the year, you're in a box. You know what I mean?"

"Yeah, Terry's!" Fitzy joked.

"Shutup, Fitz," Paul murmured.

"You're in a hot room, and then you walk into another hot room, and then you run out to your car and start it up and turn the heat on . . . you just move from box to box. Start feeling . . . strangulated or something. But in the summer—the windows are open, the doors are open. You just pass from the inside to the outside and back again. The whole world is your box, you know? You can breathe. Your skin feels better. The crickets. Everything.

"They had this community garden up there—"

"We used to throw the horse shit on it in the winter," Sully said, pulling his finger down from his nose.

"In between the main dormitory and the chapel, and out back a bit. Shady Oaks is on a hill, and the wind's always blowing, especially in winter, but this garden was protected by a wall of bushes, like three stories high."

"Yeah," Paul remembered.

"Planted on the north side of the garden and the two sides like. So you couldn't really see behind you when you were working in the garden. But looking out—anyone remember that view? How unbelievable? Way up high, and protected, and the whole world thrown out before you, rolling hills and valleys and farms and what have you. Anyway, it was one of my favorite places to be. That was probably the chore up there I liked best. We only had to be in the garden like one day a week, but I used to trade my days with some of the other guys who hated it out there, so I'd be there three days a week. It was amazing; every day I'd go out there and something new had happened. Something had grown a foot, and something else had started bearing fruit . . . I don't know. I loved it. But this night turned out to be quite auspicious."

"What the fuck does that mean?" Fitzy chorused.

"Something happened. It was a night to remember," Paul explained rapidly. "Shut the fuck up, Fitz."

"It was one of these summer nights after Lights Out, but I couldn't sleep—way too hot. It was the full moon that night, or close enough that it didn't matter if it wasn't. I was lying in my bed, sweating—I had the top bunk and all the heat in the room was stuck up by the ceiling—and I was watching the moonlight on the floor, like . . . spilled silver. Shifting, rolling. Like milk. Then there'd be like a cloud smudge, and the light would fade, it would be pitch-dark in a heartbeat. Then all bright again. Finally I got up, a lather of sweat. I pulled on a pair of gym shorts and my sneakers and decided to pop out for a breath of air."

"Don't worry. It's gonna get real good," I heard Paul whisper to the guy next to him, who I didn't know. He was from some room down the hall.

"My eyes really didn't get used to the dark until I slipped behind the hedge and came out into the garden. And then I could see what had been smudging the light out. These big navy and gray clouds were sailing across the sky. Slow, slow, like them huge oil barges we'd see out in the harbor, remember them? And as they'd float across the moon, these cloud-ships would change colors, it was like they went into an X-ray machine and you could see at last what they were made of. Not navy and gray at all, but blue, and white, and yellow at the edges, and everything would get pitch-dark when they came to the middle. And then that particular one would pass, and the world was all silver again. Except for the shadows, which were so black they were purple.

"It was when the light came out again that I saw her. Terry. She wasn't there when the moon went in, but when it came out she was standing there, right at the edge of the garden. Straight and tall and still as the corn plants, which were shoulder high by then. The moon was behind her. When it came out, it lit up her shoulders, the sides of her hair, it like silhouetted her. And I . . . I started to Believe again."

I paused.

"Believe?" Fitzy asked. "Believe in what?"

Everybody raised their head to me. They held their breaths.

"Everything," I said again.

Fitzy opened his mouth to say *Bullshit,* I could see the lips gather to make and thrust that "b" sound out into this world. But instead he paused and his breathing grew nostril-flarey.

I should say that Fitzy is a cynic.

When Fitzy was a kid people used to stop his mother—who was kinda a hippie-freak and had let Fitzy's hair grow long—to tell her her little kid in the stroller looked just like *The Light of the World,* some baby picture of Jesus some artist painted. One time when he got busted for DUI, there was a lady cop there and as they shoved Fitzy into the back of the cruiser she recognized him and said, "Hey, I re-member when you were *The Light of the World.*"

Fitzy looked up at her handcuffed, shitfaced, and said, "You got the wrong light, lady."

You begin to understand Jesus during that moment of moments when you are not so gently get-in-there-you shoved into the rear of a police cruiser, because you have crossed that line. Otherness. Look at that person there.

"Everything," I repeated.

Fitzy stared at the space between his beat-up sneakers.

"So what happened?" Paul asked, and he was leaning forward so far in his chair, for once he was forgetting to crack his knuckles. Every-one's eyes were on me.

"I was staring at Terry, the moon behind. A silhouette that you want to fill in with everything you ever hoped for. When my eyes got a little more used to the dark I could see she was staring at her watch.

"'What . . . what time is it?' I whispered to her. We were twenty feet away from each other.

"'Ssshhhh,' she whispered back, gently, lovingly, holding up a finger. 'I'm taking the night's pulse,' she said.

"'I don't understand you', I said. I'm a very ignorantish person."

"'You can tell the temperature from the crickets,' she said. 'You can. Like a dog, like a lot of things, they breathe faster or slower depending on how hot it is. There's a formula, there is. You count the number of cricket chirps you hear in fourteen seconds, and add forty to that number. And that's the temperature.'

"We stepped closer to each other. I thought I might choke on the desire that was inside my throat, swelling up inside the top part of my chest like a balloon being blown up inside there.

"'How hot is it?' I whispered, and the moon went behind a cloud again and the night got underwater and purple-velvety again.

"'Hot,' she said. 'It's very hot.'

"'I don't know if I can do this again,' I told Terry. 'Don't know if I can survive if I keep doing this.'"

"Huh?" Fitzy said.

"So intense," I said. "Or maybe I meant couldn't survive without it, I meant both and Terry knowing everything I didn't say. She was right in front of me now; we were right in front of each other. I could feel her breath on my bare skin. The prickles that leapt up to eat her breath.

"'I read something once,' Terry murmured in a husky voice. 'There is no problem to which love is not the solution.'"

"What were you wearing? What was she wearing?" Sully asked, his breath coming fast like mine was that night, like ours was.

My eyes met everybody's and everything else fell away except this recitation of Passion, this sharing of a part of being human, the throbbing of things.

"Me, just gym shorts. Sneakers. Unfortunately they were smelly."

"What about Terry?" Fitzy blurted.

"Terry was just wearing a T-shirt and cutoff dungaree shorts. A V-neck very white T-shirt, and dungaree shorts with little strands of thread dangling down here and there, little fray forays onto those soft legs, that soft skin like rose petals."

An irrepressible moan wiggled up from somewhere in the back of the room.

"'How hot?' I whispered to Terry in front of me, the all of her now.

"'It's very hot,' Terry said. 'Eighty-eight degrees. Very hot. I'm sweating everywhere.'" She paused to stare. "I want you to count the beads of sweat on me. I want you to lick them all off me everywhere.'"

"Oh, Jesus," Paul mumbled. Fitzy started coughing; he'd swallowed his gum, I think. Sully was just sitting there sweating, his eyes burning. He'd gone jogging again earlier; I could actually smell him even up here at the front of the room.

"Terry lifted up her arms over her head, the way a little kid will when their mother's about to undress them."

I gulped and shuddered.

"Even now," I said, "even now remembering it, it's like I have to stare hard into the heart of that memory before I can see it, everything is still blurry and melty with the heat of that night, how hot it was, how hot what we were about to do was. It's like them pigeons that would roost on the roof of the Projects, remember, Fitzy? How at night we'd go up to the roof and the pigeons would be behind the door fluffering and feathery-shuddering, and you couldn't see them that good in the night, just a fluttered wing here and there, a hopping, but you could hear and smell them doing that? That's how this memory is, even now, a blurry silhouette I want to fill in again."

"Was s-she wearing a bra?" Ed from next door asked and his voice cracked. He was still a virgin at twenty-two and took a lot of ribbing for that. He looked like he didn't know whether to shit or go blind, as we used to say.

"Oh no, she never wore no bra," I answered.

"What were her tits like? Did you tit-fuck her?" Fitzy wanted to know.

"Go," Paul mumbled. "Go, keep going."

"I lifted her shirt up, and off. Her hair got tousled, the moonlight explored it and found different places in it it could light up. She un-buttoned her cutoffs and they plunged to the ground. The noise of them I still can remember, and the hot-puffy breeze found strange places between my legs when I did the same. We were naked now ex-cept for our shoes. I licked her arms, fell down, fell, licked a spot I didn't know about before, some place on her side just above, just be-low, the side of her waist. Wanted to sail up and down that coast there forever lost at sea and found like never before."

"So what happened?" Fitzy whined, his face all flushing.

"You were lickin' her," Sully said. "You were lickin' her and what did she do?"

"'Oh, everything now,' Terry whispered, 'everything and every-thing and everything. But not here, over here, over here come, come.'

"She yanked my hand and I could feel the throbbing of it. Night-thudding. Wildness jumped between us. A tang you could almost smell and lick like wildgoat. She yanked me stumbling over to one side of the garden, this small patch they'd just plowed over all black and thick and fertile-like, yards of compost they'd chucked onto it. Our toes plunge-sank into its warm mucky-muck. We fell down, sunk into it, rolled and moiled. The moon looked for a second a beam-stab but its light fuzzy and dotty at the smeared edges of it, then it saw what we were doing and all went blackness again and the night like hot purple syrup. She slid the ooze all over me, gathery handfuls of the smell smeared on my ass and my glidey back and the sides of my chest, the rib meat attached. Spinning and revolving and evolving until so black above me I couldn't tell when she was on top then me, we were both on top and both below. I was looking at the sky and then the grass the next second and both so black that sky and earth became one with me and Terry-Love.

"She was sitting up half sunk in the earth and me standing pronged before her and yanked me by hands on my ass into her mouth, took me into the slippery opening like it had been born to get in there and my muddy hands on her head back and forth like that and me looking to the sky and roaring silently then back down to see her in the darkness feasting like that, her legs an open V and the quads all wide and flexed and white and strong."

"Talk slower," Paul whispered, both his hands on his lap.

"And then her leaning over, looking away, one hand crawling away and beside us to where the vegetables grow, plucking cucumbers off the teepee bush she is.

"'I want to see you like that,' she mumbles, her mouth full up, 'want you to feel what that's like,' and then she took a cucumber and into my mouth with it, in and out with it, and then she shoved another in, and then tried to do a third but I was slobbering replete."

"Jesus, Danny," Paul mumbled and the rest of them were half-open with their mouths except for Fitzy who was looking down, remembering I figgered Judy what-was-her-last-name-night, that fat Projects girl who used Gee Your Hair Smells Terrific shampoo who used to let the two or three or four of us fuck her. Her mother worked nights and one time when she fell asleep with me and Fitz on either side of her bare, fat ass he reached over and grabbed me that time.

"The rumble of the thunder then, way off across the valley and behind its hidden veils reverberating and you picture the people there in their dark-wallpapered rooms, in their rumply, hot beds and the rain running down hills and gutters and it's a-walking this way.

"'Cum all over me,' Terry said, 'Spray me over and over everywhere as many times as you can——'"

"*Uuh, uh, ohhhhh!*" Sully cried out as he came, this time seemingly without touching himself, though you never knew with Sully; he was sly. And this time no one laughed because they wished they could.

"Lights out, gentlemen!" and no one moved an inch. Then everybody was talking at once, some of them shouting as they vaulted up.

"What kinda build does Terry like? Does she mind if you smoke? What if you have a slip? Will she stick by you 'til you get sober and sane again?" But when we finally got everyone out of the room and shut the door Paul hadn't moved from his chair and he was shaking, looking down at the floor.

"What about if you kill somebody!" he sobbed when it finally broke out.

"There is no problem to which love is not the solution," I said. And Sully, shocked, staring behind him, reached out his hand and rested it on Paul's shoulder while he wept. The wet spot on Sully's shorts coming through was like his tenderness finally being born again.

Another knock on the door, and it's someone I don't know, from the other side of the building.

"Tomorrow night again?" he asked.

"Yes," I said. "Tomorrow night again and every night until we're out of here."

WE HAD THIRTY-SEVEN nights left as of that night, I remember. I told them about Terry Love for thirty-five of them nights. One night I was sick, stomach bug, and couldn't do it; the other night I needed a break. On both nights they met next door; I could hear them through the wall, recounting their favorite Terry moments from my stories.

WE "GRADUATED" a little over a month later—a dubious booby-prize term, graduating from a detox center, but, really, no tasseled know-it-all has ever been prouder. They said, and would say, years after, that no "class" had ever done better. Only one out of sixty-four of us didn't make it when the sluice opened that would spill us back into Life. It's someone you don't know so you don't have to worry about it, but he was angel-faced and one time I saw him still, intently looking at a bird singing down to him from a tree out back here, and don't ask me what kind of tree it was, and he extended a finger that had fought and stole and poisoned himself with booze and he held his breath and cooed whimpering in words I couldn't hear to get the bird to land on that small piece of finger he was extending into the world. For about an hour, and me watching him unknown. But it never did. Kind of ironic that he killed himself by launching his lean booze-pickled body off a five-story apartment building onto the parking lot below. Unless he found some other world on his way down.

Listen, this is what happened.

Paul. He never left with us. They offered him a job and he's still up there, assistant director by now and with a doctorate or whatever they call it if you can believe it. I saw him on a local cable talk show one night, debating about some pilot program that needed funding with a cheap fuck-fat Republican from somewhere out in the sticks. Handsome as ever, Pauly-Boy, and nary a knee-bounce, though of course you'd think everyone would get nervous in front of them hot lights. He did crack his knuckles once though. When I laughed at that, Terry next to me in bed half-asleep smiled and asked *"What?"*

Sully does triathlons now, those running-swimming-biking things. In fact, he runs one every year on the South Shore now to raise money for a new alcohol treatment center for kids he wants to set up next to the projects back home. He had a slip once. Took the money and went on a boozin' spree of girly-wildness down to one of them Indian gambling places they got way in the woods in Connecticut there. But in spite of what you might've heard, Southie is a forgiving place, and now sober again he's almost got enough money again to open the place, except now his Aunt Teresa the ex-nun holds all the money for him and you will recall, if you know her at all, that St. Peter himself could not get a dime out of that one if it cost that much to get into heaven.

Fitzy. Fitzy finished his heating ventilation air conditioning training and got a really good job with the government up in Maine. He met a nice girl and they got three kids now. He takes pride, as well he should, in being utterly mundane. "We're going to Sears this afternoon to buy shit if you can believe it," he told me a month ago over the phone, laughing. "I fuckin' love it."

BUT GETTING BACK to our last day there. A Sunday morning it was, early September. The sky like that, endless and blue, and the light going all tender through things, trees, patches of grass. A shed that you'd never look at otherwise. There's a bus right outside back to town. You know, it goes right by Shady Oaks too on the way back to Southie, back to the civilization that is waiting to crunch, seething as it waits to make us other people's snarly animals again. It's funny—

the worse you get, the farther out they send you, is what I'm saying, this bus. Sully had gone to church. Did I tell you that about Sully, how he went to church every Sunday? They were holding our bus for him, and the sound of the bells and him came drifting up the hill, but Sully never ran. Smiling, showing off those new pearly whites he'd gotten at the infirmary his last week here.

"Where the *fuck* were you?" Fitzy asks as the bus rumbles off. We're all a little nervous. Paul waves good-bye and then he's gone. But some are more nervous than others. It's not just this new life I'm starting, this whole new life, this whole new world—

—it's they all want to meet Terry when we pull through her little town there right where Shady Oaks is, where I'll be getting off forever. That little town, and Big Terry.

"Lucky you," Fitzy says twenty times, while I comb my hair in the reflected glass window, do five hundred push-ups in the bouncy aisle to let loose a lot of tension because they all want to meet her, to see her.

"She might not be there," I say when we whiz by the sign that says ENTERING RUTLAND. "She said she might have to work today."

"Where, at the stables?" Sully asks.

"Yeah, yeah, the stables," I say. "The stables. Or maybe making furniture there where she works. Her workshop at home there."

"She won't be there?" Sully asks. "She's waitin' for you and she won't be there?"

"I . . . dunno," I say. "I dunno, I dunno. She mentioned something about sending her brother if she couldn't make it herself."

"I can't believe she wouldn't be there to meet you, Danny," Fitzy says. "She ain't the Terry you made us believe she is if she can't come down to meet you."

"I dunno," I say. I fold my arms and swallow hard. The bus takes a mean bounce, a lurch, and I wait for it to start going again but it doesn't. The snake-hiss of air brakes, then "Rutland!" says the bus driver. "Anyone for Rutland?" And my eyes narrow and blind for a second with the turmoil of it all. I jump up, grab my hockey duffel bag from the rickety rack above me, and lurch forward to the front of the bus. Then I stop and turn around; I've forgotten to say good-bye.

But Fitzy and Sully are doubled up at the window like little kids, noses pressed, looking out.

"Is that her?" Sully asks, pointing an unbitten finger.

"Naw, that can't be her," Fitzy says. "No tits on that one, and lookit the defeated look about her, no?"

"Ahh . . . see you guys," I say.

They both turn. We stare. Mountains pass between us, but I can't stay. We shake hands, a cryptic neighborhood handshake that we laugh at, yeah, we still remember. Fitzy has tears in his eyes and we end up hugging hard like that.

I turn around and head back up to the front of the bus. An old lady is lifting herself onto the bus, carefully, smelling of summery dusting powder and carrying a world within a bake-shop box, all done up with miles of that cordy, happy string they have. She smiles and then I book it down the steps when she finally plops down with a delighted sigh.

I stop on the sidewalk, snap-look around. My breath's coming in jags—

"Danny! *Danny! Over here!*"

If I can only not cry as I fall into the arms of Terry I still might be able to pull this off. I half-open an eye, still wrapped up with Terry, as the bus smears passed. Sully and Fitzy's face are a blur.

A WEEK LATER after a meeting I call Sully from a pay phone down on three-block long Main Street. Just to see how he's doing, tell him how good I'm doing. I keep grub-shoving quarters in 'til I'm broke again. We laugh, we talk. We talk.

After I hang up the phone I start walking home to where I live now, to where we live. I go up the hill. The world gets bigger with every lurch. That smell of things. Flowing down all through me, horses and hay fields and something else that's new and open. Like the view now in front of me.

I've missed the sunset over the valley by about ten minutes, but the sky's all orange and big and everything, and I have to stop for a minute, I have to. I pluck a piece of grass from the side of the road, stick it in my mouth, chew. Think a little.

I didn't drink today. That's such a good thing. Terry's working on a bureau for someone out in the workshop and later tonight in the bedroom there will be that smell that I don't notice anymore because I am now part of the smell.

I don't know, man. I might have to, like, reassess my opinion of Sully. I don't think he's as prejudiced as I assiduously assumed he was.

I start whistling this song, break into a trot, home.

ABOUT THE AUTHOR

Joe Hayes, a writer and teacher, is the author of the critically acclaimed short story collection, *This Thing Called Courage: South Boston Stories* (2002).

Order a copy of this book with this form or online at:
http://www.haworthpress.com/store/product.asp?sku=5174

NOW BATTING FOR BOSTON
More Stories by J. G. Hayes

_____in softbound at $16.95 (ISBN-13: 978-1-56023-522-4; ISBN-10: 1-56023-522-5)

Or order online and use special offer code HEC25 in the shopping cart.

COST OF BOOKS_____

☐ **BILL ME LATER:** (Bill-me option is good on US/Canada/Mexico orders only; not good to jobbers, wholesalers, or subscription agencies.)
☐ Check here if billing address is different from shipping address and attach purchase order and billing address information.

POSTAGE & HANDLING_____
(US: $4.00 for first book & $1.50 for each additional book)
(Outside US: $5.00 for first book & $2.00 for each additional book)

Signature_____

SUBTOTAL_____

☐ **PAYMENT ENCLOSED: $**_____

IN CANADA: ADD 7% GST_____

☐ **PLEASE CHARGE TO MY CREDIT CARD.**

STATE TAX_____
(NJ, NY, OH, MN, CA, IL, IN, PA, & SD residents, add appropriate local sales tax)

☐ Visa ☐ MasterCard ☐ AmEx ☐ Discover
☐ Diner's Club ☐ Eurocard ☐ JCB

Account # _____

FINAL TOTAL_____
(If paying in Canadian funds, convert using the current exchange rate, UNESCO coupons welcome)

Exp. Date_____

Signature_____

Prices in US dollars and subject to change without notice.

NAME_____
INSTITUTION_____
ADDRESS_____
CITY_____
STATE/ZIP_____
COUNTRY_____ COUNTY (NY residents only)_____
TEL_____ FAX_____
E-MAIL_____

May we use your e-mail address for confirmations and other types of information? ☐ Yes ☐ No
We appreciate receiving your e-mail address and fax number. Haworth would like to e-mail or fax special discount offers to you, as a preferred customer. **We will never share, rent, or exchange your e-mail address or fax number.** We regard such actions as an invasion of your privacy.

Order From Your Local Bookstore or Directly From
The Haworth Press, Inc.
10 Alice Street, Binghamton, New York 13904-1580 • USA
TELEPHONE: 1-800-HAWORTH (1-800-429-6784) / Outside US/Canada: (607) 722-5857
FAX: 1-800-895-0582 / Outside US/Canada: (607) 771-0012
E-mail to: orders@haworthpress.com

For orders outside US and Canada, you may wish to order through your local
sales representative, distributor, or bookseller.
For information, see http://haworthpress.com/distributors

(Discounts are available for individual orders in US and Canada only, not booksellers/distributors.)
PLEASE PHOTOCOPY THIS FORM FOR YOUR PERSONAL USE.
http://www.HaworthPress.com   BOF04